What About the Girl?

What About the Girl?

KT Cavan

What About the Girl?
By KT Cavan

Published by Asp
An imprint of IndieBooks

ISBN: 978-1-908041-71-5

© 2021 IndieBooks Limited

Set in Times 11/12
Cover design by Jem Butcher
Cover Illustration by Jacqueline Bissett

Printed by TJ Books Ltd, Padstow PL28 8RW

1

Clemency gazed out over the spires and towers and jumbled red roofs of the city of Bern. Though the steel bars meant she could only open the window a crack, she could feel the summer heat and imagine the scent of Alpine meadows. It was the kind of day to be rowed around the lake in the park or driven out into the countryside in an open-top sports car, with a picnic of cold chicken and salad and chilled white wine.

How unfortunate, then, that there was no-one in her life to do the rowing or the driving. In any case her shift would last well into the evening.

Behind her, the teletype machine began to chatter out its secrets.

1415Z TELNO 4743 SECRET FOREIGN OFFICE LONDON TO UKMIS GENEVA COPY UKDEL NATO PARIS WASHINGTON MOSCOW BONN BERN SUBJECT ARMS REDUCTION NEGOTIATIONS ROUND FOUR YOUR TELNO 4704 23 JUNE 1962 REQUESTING CONFIRMATION ON SOVIET BLOC INTENTIONS FOR INTERMEDIARY RANGE MISSILES...

She sighed. Last weekend, Simon and Gail Pemberton, who had a chalet across the French border in St Quentin, had organised a picnic in a meadow above the village. The Embassy people were a bit dull, except for Major Aspinal, of course, but it had still been fun. She'd played with the two young Pembertons, which made her a friend of Gail and saved her from too much chat about schools and servants with the Embassy wives. Then, after lunch, Mrs Dansby-Gregg had cornered her and been terribly indiscreet as usual, confiding that the only way to stay sane in Bern was to have an *affaire*, and even pointing out a nearby woodcutter's hut as an ideal rendezvous.

But even if Clemency had wanted that, there was precious little chance. As the newest and youngest member of the Embassy staff, she was expected to volunteer for more than her share of the evening and weekend shifts. Perhaps it would be better once the summer was over. Except then, instead of Alpine meadows, she would be pining for the ski slopes.

The bars on the Registry windows were intended to keep the KGB from breaking in; but there were times she felt they were there to stop her from getting out.

A bell rang as the machine came to a halt. She tore off the paper and went back to her desk to type the telegram out afresh: a white original for the Ambassador and carbon copies on pink or blue flimsy paper for the desk officers.

'Whose turn is it to make tea?'

The question came from Annabelle, the senior of the three registry clerks, so perfect in her accent, her pearls and twin-set, that she was known throughout the building as the Duchess.

'I'll go in a minute,' Clemency replied, over the clatter of her typewriter.

Joy emerged from the Registry room, where the Embassy's records were secured behind a heavy steel door. She always complained about working there because she thought the old-book smell of the files got into her hair. Soon, Clemency would offer to take over, to keep her sweet and for a little variety. Handling Britain's most sensitive secrets could be a bore.

'Good morning, ladies.'

It was typical of Peter Aspinal to appear silently in the open doorway, leaning against the lintel and watching the three of them at their work. So too the lazy smile and the appraising gaze.

'Major.' It was Annabelle who spoke first, her voice carefully without expression, as if to keep him firmly in his place. All part of the game.

'Come to help?' Joy asked, a little breathless.

'Come *for* help, to be precise,' he replied. The drawl matched his blazer and flannel trousers and the silk cravat in the colours of his old college, the very image of the English diplomat on his day off.

'And what is it this time?' Joy asked, staking her claim to be his helper.

'There's very little to it. A quick run down to Martigny and back. I thought it might be one for the newest member of the team.'

Clemency did not look up. She knew – everyone in the Embassy knew, without it ever being discussed – that Major Peter Aspinall was more than just the Second Secretary for commercial affairs, but MI6's man on the ground in Switzerland, their very own answer to Simon Templar or James Bond. But she didn't want to make an enemy of Joy.

'As you can see,' Joy said, 'Clemency has a lot on at the moment…'

'The thing is…'

Peter parked himself on the edge of Joy's desk and leant over so his words were for her ears only.

'Well, of course if it's like that,' she said, looking pleased. 'But Clemency, it's entirely up to you. I mean, it's outside your allocated duties here.'

'Maybe if I explain to her what's involved? We could take a stroll in the park. Feed the bears. Come and find me when you've finished that telegram.'

Clemency quickly agreed. After all, it was a lovely day, and Peter was a character, and though no doubt he would soon start to bore on about the War, as everyone of his generation did sooner or later, he was still good company. Good looking, too, for all that he must be nearly forty. And he kept in shape. If she'd been one for falling for older men, she might have been in danger.

Half an hour later he was guiding her gallantly over the road and through the entrance to the Tierpark. Despite the sunshine, it was not too busy and most of the visitors were women with young children, with a few old men sitting watching them.

'Is this your first posting?' Peter asked, making conversation.

'Yes, except for ten weeks in Paris to cover for illness.'

'And why the Foreign Office? Is it a family thing?'

'Not at all. My father's a surgeon. I think if anything he'd have wanted me to be a nurse, like Mummy. But I wanted to do something different before I settled down.'

'See the world?'

'If you like. I've always been good at languages, and when I applied they decided that as I was good at maths as well, they'd put me on the coding course. And here I am.'

They reached a quiet part of the park, away

from the river, no-one within fifty feet. Peter's tone changed.

'What I'm going to tell you is not to be shared with anyone. Not friends or family. Not with your boyfriend, if you have one. Not with Joy, or Annabelle, or even the Head of Chancery. Just you and me. This might sound like some kind of cheap radio thriller, but the fact is that we do have clandestine networks gathering intelligence in Europe, and from time to time I'm asked to help out. I had some involvement with the cloak and dagger brigade during the war and they like to keep these things within the old boys' net when they can.'

He waited patiently while a tired young woman with a pram came slowly past them.

'It's up to me to recruit any help I need locally,' he went on. 'I could find some willing helpers from the usual sources – journalists, private investigators and prostitutes – but personally I prefer to work with people I trust.

'Usually the FO is absolutely against using diplomatic staff. But the Old Man and I go back a long way and he trusts me not to cause any embarrassment. He understands that using FO staff is better than picking up Swiss nationals from the *demi-monde* and relying on their discretion.'

'But I don't know the first thing about spying.'

'Don't worry about that. All I need is cover. If I travel around Switzerland on my own, that's suspicious. First, to the opposition – the KGB and the GRU – it's a clear signal I'm up to something interesting. And second, a man on his own, in a restaurant or a café, or on a park bench – that's an invitation to speculation. What is he there for? Who is he going to meet? But no one thinks that about a couple. They're on a date, that's all. You see?'

'So I'm your date?'

He smiled.

'There's no need to sound so suspicious. I'm not going to take you on a tour of nightclubs and revue-bars. All we might do is go to a town, sit in the park over a drink, someone comes up and asks for a light or to borrow my paper, and that's it. Contact made, and we go home again.'

'And the Ambassador is happy with this?'

'Of course. But it's entirely up to you.'

'Oh, I'm fine to help. It just all seems so... I don't know. Not part of my life.'

'You spend your days decoding secret telegrams.'

'Yes, but that's working at a desk. This is the real thing.'

They had reached the Bärengraben. The bear was the symbol of Bern, standing fierce and rampant on the city's shield. In real life, the nearest animal was lying supine on a rock, one paw half-raised towards the summer sun.

'That's the life, eh?' Peter said.

'I'd rather be cold and free.'

'Would you?' He seemed to read more meaning into this than Clemency had intended. 'I wonder sometimes about the younger generation. Maybe Communism doesn't seem much of a threat. Disarmament, Aldermaston, and all that.'

Clemency decided it wasn't the time to mention that, the year before, she had joined one of the Aldermaston marches.

'I don't have any illusions about the Russians,' she said. 'Maybe it's difficult, growing up with the

Bomb. You want to be free of it. And protesting at least makes you think that could happen one day.'

'Well, luckily that kind of beatnik philosophy isn't for me. I've a job to do, and that makes it simple. Maybe for you too. If you want to do it?'

She didn't need to think.

'Of course. When do I start?'

2

The first test of Clemency's skills as an undercover agent came from Hester, her flatmate, who wanted to know who was taking her off for the day, and was it a date, and if it were work, as Clemency claimed, then why was she thinking of wearing the princess dress with the rose pattern rather than a suit? Clemency wished she had thought of a better cover story.

Peter picked her up from outside her flat and they took the road south towards Lausanne and the north-east shore of Lake Geneva. With a scarf to protect her hair from the breeze, and sunglasses, she felt very Grace Kelly and tried to be just as aloof. But it was lovely day, and being driven fast and well was a delight, and she kept smiling.

'Enjoying yourself?'

'Am I really being paid for this?'

'You'll have some work to do when we get to Martingy.'

'Look decorative, you said?'

'A little more than that,' he replied, keeping his eyes on the road. 'I want you to make the pick-up.'

'Me?'

'This is a regular arrangement. The problem is, with anything that has a pattern, the other side can spot it. We usually meet in the park. If either of us were being followed, then the first time they may not see how the switch is made. The second or third time, they'll know for sure, and we're in trouble.'

'Do you think they know about it? The Soviets?'

'I always assume the worst.'

'Could they be following us?'

She couldn't stop herself from looking over her shoulder. The couple in the car behind seemed every bit as ordinary and she and Peter were supposed to be. She turned back to find Peter glancing at her, amused.

'I had thought of that, you know. The only way to know for sure is to try and shake them off, and that means letting them know that you're suspicious. And as we're simply on a drive in the country, there's no need for that, is there?'

'What happens when we get to Martigny?'

'That's the other reason for you making the pick-up. The usual plan would be to park up, stooge around a bit, then make the drop. But that gives the opposition too much time to try something on. We're going to be in and out before they've even found somewhere to park. I would have told you earlier, but sometimes it's better not to have too long to think about things. And it's very straightforward. Nothing to it, really.'

'It's fine. I'd like to help.'

'That's my girl. Now, this is the drill. We'll drive into the town, to the main square. I'll pull over outside a café. You run in and buy a packet of cigarettes from the counter. It's near the back of the café. Ask for Kensingtons. And when the man gives it to you, ask for a copy of the *Allegemagne Zeitsung*.'

'Then what?'

'As you turn to leave, a man will come up to you with a silk scarf in his hand. He'll say to you that he thinks you dropped it. You thank him and take it. Be careful, because there'll be a packet wrapped up in it. Just put the whole thing in your handbag, along with the cigarettes. Then come out and find me. I'll be waiting as near as I can beyond the café. You get in again, and then we're done.'

'It sounds straightforward.'

'All you have to do is act natural. You're in a rush, because I'm waiting outside. You've dropped something, so when a man hands it back to you, then you give him a big smile and say thank you, but don't hang around. You're a pretty girl and a quick smile is plenty. And out you come.'

'I can do that.'

'There's just one more thing. If no-one approaches you, don't wait. Come out of the café and stand on the pavement for a moment or two. Just long enough to read the headlines on the paper. You can read German, can't you?'

'I can.'

'I thought so. If he makes the pass, fine. Take the scarf and come over to the car as before. If not, then come to the car but don't get in. Just open the door and pass me the paper. That way I'll know it hasn't worked, and I'll get out of the car and join you.'

'What then?'

He laughed.

'I have no idea. It's fatal to plan too much ahead. Probably we'll go and do a bit of sightseeing and come back to the café twenty minutes later. Then give him another chance. But it all depends on the mood. If it feels like something's wrong, we'll just have to be on our way and find another time to make contact.'

They passed a sign: Martigny was just fifteen kilometres away.

'Tell me a bit more about yourself. What did you do between school and joining the Office?'

'Me? I went up to London and rattled around for a bit.'

'And what does rattling around for a bit involve?'

'Oh, well, I stayed with a friend in a flat in Maida Vale and did lots of silly jobs for a year. Someone I met worked as a stagehand at Drury Lane and before I knew it I was an assistant dresser. It was the lowest of the low and I was laying out shoes and ironing – they wouldn't trust me with costumes or wigs – but all sorts of famous people would be popping in and out. So that was at night, and then during the day I was a waitress in the Gingham Café on Wardour Street. Do you know it? They have it decked out like an American diner, and we had these college sweaters like cheerleaders, and little gingham skirts, and we were on roller skates. Can you imagine it? Rolling around serving cakes and coffee. One time, one of the boys caught me by the hem of my skirt and pulled me back, and because I was on wheels, I couldn't do anything about it. I did feel a fool.'

'Sounds fun,' Peter replied dryly, as if confirming all his worst ideas about Swinging London.

'How did you become a spy?' she asked.

'The war. Afterwards, they wanted a few people to stay on. I'd seen some of what the Russians were capable of, so I thought it was the right thing to do. And here I am.'

'Do you have a gun?'

'It's in there.' He nodded to the glove compartment.

'Really? Can I see?'

'Yes, but be careful with it.'

She took out the pistol, sitting snug in its plain leather case. Most of all, she was surprised by the weight of it.

'It's a Beretta 70,' Peter said. 'It takes seven rounds of 7.65mm Browning short. Some people get very precious about guns. From my point of view, it looks like it means business and if I want it to, it will go bang. If you have to show anyone a gun, things have already gone wrong; and if you have to fire it, all you want is for the other person to keep their head down while you beat a hasty retreat.'

She grinned.

'I'm sure you take it more seriously than that.'

'Of course. Like any tool, I know how to use it properly and I look after it. In fact, I'll show you one day. Have you ever fired a pistol?'

'Me?'

'Don't be so shocked. There's nothing to it, really. We'll go down to the range and you can try it out. I'd be interested in what you think of it.'

She looked at the gun, heavy in her lap.

'I'd like that.'

Before they had set out, she hadn't been sure how seriously he took her. Her role was supposed to be decorative. Then he had decided that she would be making the contact. Now he was talking guns with her, as if she might understand, even have a view of her own. And the thought that he had fought in the war, perhaps behind enemy lines, was all the more intriguing because he hadn't talked about it.

They were approaching the outskirts of the town. There were the typical close-mown grass verges, the neat houses with their painted shutters, a few people strolling in the sunshine. More traffic, too, in front and behind. But it didn't hold them up. The café would be only a few minutes ahead.

The silence became oppressive.

'Have you noticed,' she began at random, 'how in Switzerland, even the telephone wires are more tidy? I mean, in England they droop down, or are covered in wisteria. But here they are like new.'

'I expect they have a law about it,' he replied casually, his eyes still flicking to the car behind. 'You know. Citizens must polish their telephone wires between 5pm and 7pm on the third Tuesday of the month.'

She laughed a little too much. They passed a row of shops, a church, more houses, the traffic almost at a crawl as cars scouted for somewhere to park.

'Here you go.'

The café was like any other. A few tables under a red awning; the windows in shadow, so you could see nothing inside; a few adverts for cigarettes and magazines; and the red sign that showed it sold tobacco and newspapers.

She repeated her lesson. 'A pack of Kensingtons and a *Zuidgemein*.'

'That's right.'

There was no time to linger. Cars were parked all along the pavement, so he simply stopped in the road. She checked in her bag for her purse, and then went inside. It was dark after the spring sunshine, and her nose wrinkled with the mix of cigarette smoke, cooking and spilt wine. There were more tables, a few customers chatting or reading newspapers. She went up to the counter and asked for the cigarettes, then the paper. Even before she had put her change back in her purse, a man was at her shoulder.

'Excuse me, Fraulein, but I believe you dropped this.'

'Oh, thank you, that's so kind of you.'

She had a glimpse of a tubby man, no taller than her, with a soft smile and a way of holding his head a little to one side. He could have been a clerk, or a shopkeeper: not what she had expected.

He smiled, bowed and turned away. She had the scarf in her hand, and she pushed it into her bag and made for the door. It really had been that simple.

Outside, she saw Peter's car about twenty yards along the road, pulled over in a narrow gap, and she headed towards it.

Then, all in an instant, a hand pressed hard on her shoulder as her bag was torn from her. Before she could even look up, the man was hurrying away, his coat flapping around him, her bag grasped incongruous in his hand.

At once she was on her feet and chasing after him, in time to see him duck into an alley. Everything else was forgotten: Peter, even the packet.

The man was half-running, but not in full flight: more as if he were late for a train. Had there been anyone else around, she might have called out for help, but in contrast to the main square, the side road was deserted.

She ran on, almost turned her ankle, and stopped long enough to slip off her shoes. Soon she was gaining on him.

Then another man stepped out from a doorway. Heavy-built, in a winter coat and scarf, a hat pulled down over his eyes, he seemed to fill the passage. Then she realised it was deliberate. Instead of asking for his help, she ran on towards him, then side-stepped at the last moment when he tried to grab her. Surprised, he slipped, and cursed, his arms closing on empty air.

Now she was enjoying herself. The first man ran across another road, the traffic screeching to a halt, and she followed, only a few yards behind. He glanced round and stretched out each step, but he was out of condition and she could hear his laboured breathing. And there were other people around.

'Voleur! Arretez!' Even in French, her cries sounded ridiculous. But at once a young man turned to stand in the thief's path, a hand raised. The man dodged to one side and slammed into a pram. He fell across it, the mother screamed, the baby began to wail. Clemency's bag fell to the floor, spilling its contents across the pavement. Ignoring the man, she grabbed the scarf, the packet, and her purse.

'Clemency!'

Peter was leaning out of the passenger window, waving her over.

'Just a minute,' she replied, reaching for her lipstick, her compact and her brush.

'Get in the car, you stupid bitch!'

She looked up, startled, her face as red as if he had slapped her. Then she noticed the man who had robbed her getting to his feet, shaking off the irate mother; the other man would be behind her.

She left the rest of her possessions and ran for the car. Peter leant over and dragged her in, even as he let in the clutch and the car sped away, on the wrong side of the street.

'You got it?'

'I did.'

At the next corner, he slowed, turned right and at once began to drive like a sober citizen, all the better to blend in and be forgotten. He risked a quick glance at her.

'What are you laughing for?' he asked.

'Your face,' she replied. 'Oh, I'm sorry, but you were so angry.'

'Well, of all the damn-fool things to do. Either of

them might have had a knife, or even a gun.'

'I didn't think.' She managed to suppress her smile for a moment. 'I'm very sorry.'

'No, you're not,' he snapped. Then, like a teacher who could not keep up the act any longer, he smiled. 'Never mind. No harm done. But when you took off after them like a bloody gazelle, I did wonder how on earth I was going to explain it to London.'

'Are you sure it was them?'

'You're thinking of common or garden thieves? It's a bit of a coincidence, isn't it? After all, this is Switzerland, you know. Not a lot of crime to start with.'

They were heading out of town now, towards Zurich rather than back to Bern. Peter was still wary, his eyes more on the rear-view mirror than the road.

'We'll find a café,' he said. 'Get some lunch. Then find a quiet way to trickle back home. Remember, we haven't done anything wrong. Someone stole your bag, and you ran after them, that's all. But the police might wonder why you – we – didn't stick around to answer their questions.'

'I bet someone took your number-plate.'

'I don't care, so long as we get home with the package and don't run into those Moscow types again. We have diplomatic immunity, remember. If the Swiss police complain about our running away, we'll counter-complain about being robbed in broad daylight, and all will be forgotten. But…' he broke off. 'Thought so. We have company.'

She looked back to where a black Mercedes was coming up behind them fast.

'They can't do anything, can they?'

'Not if we lose them.'

She stayed silent, letting him concentrate on the

road. He wasn't trying to outrun their pursuers. Perhaps the Mercedes was powerful enough to keep up with them, for all that they were in a sports car.

'I'm surprised they're bothering,' he said. 'Perhaps the package is a lot more important that I thought. Or perhaps they're embarrassed that they were outwitted by a girl. That won't look good in their report.'

Soon they caught up with a truck labouring up a hill. The Mercedes tucked in behind. Peter looked more thoughtful and she wondered what would happen if they were caught or driven off the road. There were at least two men, probably armed. Peter had his gun, but surely it wouldn't come to that.

Suddenly she was flung against him as they slewed across the carriageway, tyres squealing, into a side road. Behind, the Mercedes wallowed as it braked and turned to follow them.

The road was narrow, a country lane following the line of a stream, dappled by the overhanding trees. There were meadows to each side, cows, a barn, all quite charming, if you forgot the carful of hoodlums behind. Peter was driving much faster than she would ever have dared, and soon they were climbing up the side of the valley, the road switching back and forth. She couldn't help but look back, and the Mercedes was struggling to keep up. Peter was smiling, and his hands on the wheel, occasionally flicking the gearstick back and forth, were in perfect control. She began to relax, realising the plan. On the open road, the heavier engine of the Mercedes would win out. But here, the little sports car, light and with more precise steering, could take the bends far faster.

'They should have Bought British,' he called out over the sound of the engine. She sat back to enjoy the ride.

With anyone else, it would have been terrifying. The gravel spun under their wheels on every bend, and there was only a low stone wall to stop them from tumbling down the side of the mountain. But Peter was in his element. The Mercedes was falling behind. And then, as it made an effort to catch up, the inevitable happened and it skidded, recovered, crunched into the wall and then crossed the road again to end up in the ditch.

It was obvious there would be no more pursuit, but Peter hardly slowed down. He was enjoying himself too much, and perhaps showing off to her as well. Clemency decided to treat it as a roller-coaster ride: frightening, except that, deep down, you knew there was no real danger.

A while later, they were over the mountains and into the next valley. Peter eased up a bit, then took out the Michelin guide and dropped it into her lap.

'Find us a restaurant. In a village, at least an hour away. Somewhere with more than one road in and out.'

She began to search, then broke off to look at him, wondering for the first time how he had managed to find her so quickly, back in Martigny, and what would have happened if he had not. But it was not until they were sitting in the shade of a terrace, looking out over the valley of the Rhône to the snowy peaks of the Alps, a bottle of the crisp local white wine in front of them, that she asked him.

'Nothing,' he replied, not looking up from the leather-bound menu. 'Or rather, nothing more than they had to do to do their job. They might have hit you, or wrenched your arm, to stop you resisting, but all this is strictly business. One of the rules of the game is that you don't wage war on the opposition. If we were all pulling guns on each other or sticking knives in each other's ribs, the Swiss would soon get fed up and we'd all be out on our ears. So, we keep things relatively civilised. Now, I can certainly recommend the trout, and the wild boar will be local...'

His words and his attitude were a comfort; but she still felt in his debt for rescuing her; and forgiving her for putting herself – and perhaps him – in danger.

They said no more about it, and the talk was of films and music and Embassy gossip. But as they returned to the car, Peter stopped to look out over the valley.

'Would you like to do this again?'

'Lunch? Or the pick-up?'

'Both, if you like.'

3

But there was no second outing, with or without an operation at the end of it; and no expansive, celebratory lunch afterwards. She saw Peter from time to time in the corridors of the Embassy, and once glimpsed him in a café on a Saturday afternoon while she was out shopping for fabric for a new dress; but her time in the Secret Service appeared to be over. And it was Joy who was absent the same weekend as Peter, and who – from the mystery she made of it – wanted Clemency to know that she had been at Peter's side on his latest mission.

After a while, Clemency became anxious that she might have been indiscreet, or rather that he had wrongly come to that conclusion, for in truth she had told no-one, however sore the temptation. Not Hester, or her brother, not even her father, though she so wanted to mention casually in a letter that she was helping out MI6, had even tangled briefly with a Soviet agent, and come out on top. He thought her time in the Foreign Office was little more than a paid holiday and a chance to meet the right husband, and though she couldn't say much about her work, she suspected that he wouldn't have been impressed anyway. He'd been in the RAMC, attached to the 3rd Battalion of the Parachute Regiment, and for him, warfare was shattered limbs, gaping wounds, taking and holding ground against a determined enemy – not playing about with disguises and secret codes.

She wanted to return to Peter's world; but she didn't pine for it. In Bern, in the autumn of 1962, there was no shortage of fun to be had. Unattached young women from the embassies were always in demand. Hardly a night passed by without an invite to a dance, or dinner, or a film, or she'd go to the jazz club or meet up with some of Hannah's bohemian friends, and someone would have a guitar, or another would recite free-flowing poetry, and everyone would be so serious, and drink awful red wine, and talk about free love, and there might even be the sickly scent of a reefer to add to the excitement.

The *Alabama* was her favourite. The players might only be third-hand imitations of Miles Davis or Charlie Parker via London or Hamburg, but they put passion into it. And she liked the crowd. It was relaxed, no-one judging, no-one asking you which school you went to or who your parents were.

It was around nine one Saturday evening, when a boy she hardly knew, but was coming to like, had screwed up the courage to buy her a drink, that she saw Peter standing by the door, looking around, very much out of place. His gaze passed over her and didn't stop. Maybe it was the dim coloured lights. Maybe he didn't recognise her in her black sweater and cheap cotton skirt. Either way, she mouthed an apology to the boy over the blare of the sax and weaved through the crowd to meet him.

'Can we talk outside?' He was on edge and she stopped from protesting that she'd have to pay a second time to come back in. The air was chill after the warmth of the club.

'I'm so sorry to break up your evening, Clemency, but I wanted to ask a favour.'

'Like Martigny?'

'Exactly. Only it's right now. I have a little… activity

planned and circumstances have changed, and…'

He was already striding along Langgassstrasse, and she had to half-run to keep up.

'Of course, Peter. Just tell me what you want me to do.'

'Good girl. There's a party at a private house in Stadtbach. There'll be a lot of diplomats, so I can't be seen there. I need someone to go in, pick up a letter, and come out again. This is a bit more activist that I've any right to involve you in, but there we are.'

'I can't go to a party like this,' she protested.

'That's dealt with,' he replied. 'The contact is a man called Ruppel. All you need to do is come to the back door, the servants' door, and ask for Herr Ruppel. He'll come down and meet you and give you the letter. You come back to me, and we go and have a very large drink. How does that sound?'

'I like the last bit the most.'

They walked on in silence. Peter glanced at his watch.

'Sorry. Let's slow down. We're not that late. I'm the professional and I shouldn't be letting this get to me. As I said, it's a relatively simple operation. But surprisingly expensive. I don't want London to think I'm throwing their money away.'

'Who am I supposed to be?'

'A waitress called Maria. Herr Ruppel runs a catering firm. He does a lot of these kinds of parties in private homes of the wealthy and well-connected, a lot of diplomatic events, and we've worked together in the past. He's sound, but he does get nervous. He has a way to get hold of a letter I'm rather keen on reading, but not to get it out of the house. That's where you come in. Right, here we are.'

Peter had parked next to a church with a tiny paved yard around it. The overhanging trees left it in deep shadow. He took a bag from the boot of his car and then guided her to sit on a tombstone.

'It's cold, isn't it?'

'I'm sorry to say you'll be colder still in a minute. Here, take you clothes off and get into this.' He held up a dress in black cambric, with a white collar; the kind a maid or waitress would wear. He waited, back turned, as she pulled her sweater over her head and then stepped out of her skirt. He passed the dress to her, his eyes still averted. It had seen much service but was freshly laundered. Unfortunately, it was too small for her, leaving her arms sticking out of the sleeves.

'It won't matter,' Peter said, failing to suppress a smile. 'You'll only be there for a minute or two.'

'Who was it supposed to be for?'

'Someone who has apparently had a better offer for tonight. Maybe it's one of her regular clients. I can't say I care too much.'

Clemency thought of herself as modern, even worldly-wise; but Peter's casual assumption that one could hire a prostitute to help steal a letter was startling. She wondered what else his life as a spy involved.

While she tied the white apron around her, he fixed the linen cap on her head. Now she was filled with excitement. Perhaps it was the danger, or the feeling of being dressed for a performance, or his hands in her hair, strong and delicate. She let him tuck and pull the uniform into some kind of shape, until he nodded in apparent satisfaction.

'Come out of here and turn right. There's an alley on the left after twenty yards. You'll see Ruppel's van parked outside. There will be a tray of glasses in the back. Take that and go down the alley. The servants' door will be open and just walk in. The first person you see, ask them where Herr Ruppel is. If anyone asks, your name is Maria and you have the spare glasses from the van. If that doesn't satisfy them, just look stupid and keep asking for Ruppel. OK?'

'I suppose so.'

At the café in Martigny, the surprise, the idea of taking the challenge on the bounce, had made sense. Here, she felt horribly under-rehearsed. Maybe it was the costume, the feeling she didn't know her lines, wouldn't be able to pull off the part. How did waitresses act? How would they speak? Should she try some kind of accent? But there wasn't time to ask.

They came to the edge of the churchyard, where the lights turned the cobbled street into a stage.

'I wouldn't ask you to do this if it didn't matter. If you can't pull it off, then we're no worse off. But if you can, then London will be extremely pleased. And I'll make sure the Ambassador knows too – informally.'

'And you'll come to the police station if I'm arrested?'

He leaned close.

'That's not going to happen. But I'm with you all the way on this, Clemency.'

She remembered how she had felt, watching him whispering to Joy. She turned her head to reply, touching his cheek to guide her lips to his ear.

'I'll hold you to that.'

It wasn't what she had wanted to say, but it would do.

◊

To begin with, it played out just as Peter had said. She found the van, the glasses, the open door. There was warm light slipping into the night, the sound of music and laughter coming from above, and standing outside was a tall, well-muscled man with a squashed face who clearly wasn't a guest, despite his dinner jacket and bow tie. But he hardly gave her a glance as she passed inside, the glasses chinking together cheerfully.

A younger man with sleeked black hair approached her along a narrow corridor and led her into a cramped and busy pantry, all plates of canapés and empty bottles, and up to Herr Ruppel. He was a sad-looking man with a bald dome of a head and an air of apology.

'Maria? It is Maria, isn't it?' he asked less certainly, as he peered at her more closely. At least, Clemency told herself, I don't look like a prostitute pretending to be a waitress.

'I'm afraid I have bad news,' he said quietly, after guiding her to one side. 'I must ask you to inform Herr Aspinal that the arrangement we agreed is not one that I can complete.'

'Oh,' she said blankly. 'Why is that?'

'Allow me to show you,' he said, eager to excuse himself from personal blame. 'It is that the boy who was to have made the entry and retrieved the letter is not here. *Masern*.'

She blinked. The word meant nothing.

'*Masern*. Sick with the spots,' Herr Ruppel added, mimicking the blotches of what was presumably measles. And now he was opening up the doors of a dumb waiter and explaining that the boy was to have climbed up to the study on the top floor and taken a letter from the desk there, and brought it down for Herr Ruppel to give to her to give to Herr Aspinal. With the

explanation complete, he pulled a face and stretched his
arms out, as if apologising to a client that the expected
vol au vents had been burned.

'Can't someone else go?'

She knew it was a stupid question even before she
asked it. Obviously, they had chosen the boy because
the shaft was too narrow for a man to climb. The roof
of the tiny lift had been removed, and she could peer
inside and crane her head to look up to a faint patch of
luminescence far above.

'Is there a light?'

Once Ruppel had passed her a torch, she could see
that it wasn't a difficult climb. The thick rope that had
been attached to the lift still hung down, there were
battens every few feet up the shaft. And before she
had really thought it through, she was hitching up her
dress and squirming into the base of the contraption and
Ruppel was both trying to dissuade her and giving her
exact instructions as to the particular letter she should
take.

The shaft was narrow, claustrophobic, made worse
by the dress that was far too tight over her shoulders.
Another inch, and she would never have been able to
twist round and free her arms to reach up to the first
batten and pull herself upright. But the afternoons in
the gym at school, swarming up ropes to the ceiling,
had not been wasted. She was soon coated in dust and
cobwebs – the lift had clearly been out of use for years
– but within a few minutes she was at the top, rubbing
her elbow where she had caught it on the side of the
shaft. Then she glanced down into the depths, to a pale
blob that might have been Herr Ruppel's anxious face
peering up.

She opened the sliding door of the lift. Beyond, it was

dark, silent, and heavy with the scent of wood-smoke, cigars, leather, books. Almost an animal smell; the lair of a beast that would turn savage if disturbed.

But it was empty. And there was the heavy desk, the evening's post placed neatly on one corner, just as Ruppel had said it would be.

Peter would be getting anxious. She lowered herself to the floor and moved lightly over to the desk, placing her feet carefully. Now it was Madame Weiss's dance classes that she was reliving.

The letter she was after had a Zermatt frank. But the cancellation marks were blurred, and there were a dozen or more letters to check, and all the time she was sure she could hear, against the background of the party two floors below, the sound of approaching footsteps.

There were three it could be. She crossed to the window, peered at each in turn in the light from the street lamps, angling them to try and decode the smudges of ink, cursing the Swiss post office for uncharacteristic sloppiness.

She had it, and slipped it into the pocket of the dress. But something prevented her from gliding at once to the comparative safety of the hoist.

One of the other letters; there was something odd about it. Yet also familiar.

It was a normal envelope; but inside, it felt like nothing more than a thin sheet of tracing paper: the kind she used every day for decoding telegrams.

She held it over the bulb of her torch. It was hard to be sure, but it looked like blocks of text. Five letters to a block. A code.

For a moment, she felt angry. If only Peter had explained more about why she was here, she could decide if this was a golden opportunity or a blunder that would ruin his whole operation. It shouldn't be down to her to guess.

She thought it through. If she left it, that was the end of it. But if she took it, and that was the wrong thing to do, the letter could still be put back in the post unopened, and would eventually turn up, and hopefully look like it had been misdirected.

The second letter went into her pocket.

She resisted the temptation to do any more, to look over the papers on the desk, or try and memorise names or dates in the diary of this mysterious suspect. Time to go.

She was half-way to the hoist when she heard the jangle of keys outside the door.

She froze. How could she have missed their approach? There were two of them, two men, talking in a low rumble as one of them fitted the key in the lock.

She ran to the hoist, conscious of every slight sound she made; the rustle of her dress; her feet on the floorboards. She slid open the doors of the hoist and swung herself in, feeling desperately for a foothold, twisting to get the doors shut again as the study door swung open and light blazed out.

'A Kummel?' one of the men asked, speaking in Swiss German. It was a strong voice, deep, used to giving orders.

'You are most kind, but no. I have already had a great deal of your hospitality.'

A younger man, but equally assured. Clemency couldn't move while they were there. These were not the kind of men who would hear a strange noise and assume it was a mouse. They would check, and find her, and then...

'When is Rudi back?' he went on.

'On the 17th. He is flying Pan American from New York.'

Now she wanted them to stay, so she could hear more of these clandestine arrangements.

'Will you meet him?'

'Of course. Would you like to join me?'

In the background, there was the sound of letters being opened and torn up.

'It is a great adventure for him. To fly the Atlantic alone, at the age of ten.'

'The stewardesses will take good care of him, Franz.'

'Oh, I know. They will spoil him, no doubt.'

Crouched in the lift shaft, Clemency felt mortification at her foolishness. But there was also relief that she hadn't heard anything secret, and soo was in less danger if she were discovered.

Then the man spoke again.

'That's odd. Nothing from Adler.'

'He is reliable?'

'Yes,' the older man said pensively, his mind elsewhere. And now Clemency wanted to be out of the shaft, out of the house. If the man suspected theft, he would turn the house upside down in a moment, and there would be no escape, and eventually she would be found. And what help could Peter be then?

'Is the letter important?'

'We are at a delicate stage. Anyway, here are the amendments to the contract. If you could let me have your views?'

Still there was no movement from the two men, and she could picture the older one standing by his desk, dissatisfied, his instincts telling him that something was wrong. That was how Peter would be. An experienced agent must have that skill. Peter would be thinking it though: the catering firm in the house; the abandoned dumb waiter. Peter would be approaching, making no sound, a gun in one fist. Then the hoist doors flung open, a hand of iron grasping her arm and dragging her out, to lie before the two of them, helpless.

There was a burst of laughter from below.

'Come.'

As if summoned, the two men crossed the room. Two sets of footsteps, she was sure of that. Then the door closed, the click of the lock, and more footsteps on the stairs.

She wasted no time in descending the shaft, but twice her shivering muscles let her down and she almost fell. She moved by feel and it seemed like an eternity until hands grabbed her ankles and guided her feet to the bottom of the hoist, then helped her into the kitchen.

'Quick!' Herr Ruppel hissed, brushing down her dress while she wiped the cobwebs from her face. 'The gangster they have on the door has just come looking around. I think he suspects something.'

She wanted a glass of water. Then, seeing a tray of champagne on the nearest table, she drank down a glass in one go. The bubbles made her splutter, but she felt much better.

'So. Here.'

Ruppel handed her a tray of empty glasses, her passport out again, and bustled her to the back door.

There was a flare of light as the guard lit a cigarette. She hurried past with a brief smile, hardly needing to play the part of a tired and harassed waitress.

'Miss,' the man called to her.

She stopped. Should she drop the glasses and run? The whole point was that the owner of the house should not know of the theft of the letter. And while she hesitated the man came up to her.

'Your dress.'

Clemency twisted and saw in dismay a tear across the back.

'*Merde,*' she said. 'Another night of sewing.'

'You should buy a new one. I can see too much of you in this one.'

'On what they pay me?'

'You want to make a little extra?'

Oh Christ, she thought. He does think I'm a prostitute.

'Maybe another night.'

'You look good when you're flushed. Ask for me at the Café Terminus. I'll make it worth your while.'

'OK, but you will be paying for the best.'

She used his burst of laughter to make off, dumping the glasses and then half-running back to the churchyard.

There was no-one there.

Peter had said that if he had gone, she should make her own way home. Perhaps he was waiting for her there.

She set off towards the old town, conspicuous in her costume. If they discovered the theft, and asked questions, and the man on the door remembered the girl who left early, and they came looking…

There was a car behind her, approaching fast, and she hardly had time to duck into an alley before it was next to her and Peter was leaning over and opening the passenger door.

'I seem to make a habit of this,' he said. 'What kept you?'

4

Peter's flat was in a large anonymous modern block in the Muesmatt district. As well as a front and side entrance, there was an underground car park with a lift direct to all floors, which allowed him to come and go discreetly. He waited until Clemency had admired the view, the modern furnishings and the paintings, and accepted a drink, before he allowed her to spill out her story.

When she reached the part about the shaft he couldn't hold back.

'What the hell were you thinking of? I told you to pick up a letter at the door.'

'Yes, but the boy—'

'I don't give a sod about the boy. You should have turned around and come straight back.'

'Yes, but I got the letter—'

In one move, he grabbed her, twisted her round, and had his other arm wrapped around her neck.

'Feel that? These people have the same training I do. If they decided to break your charming neck for you, it's that easy.'

She stared at him, wide-eyed.

'You're scared, right? Well, don't forget that feeling. They'd kill you and never give it another thought. That's why I'm so angry with you, Clemency. It's because I'm frightened. You're safe now but you probably came as close to being killed tonight as ever in your life. Do you see?'

She managed a tiny nod. Her eyes were filling with

tears. He led her over to the sofa and sat her down.

'I'm sorry,' he said. 'This isn't your fault. I'm the one who's been criminally stupid. Da Silva is perfectly capable of killing anyone he caught spying on him. If you'd been found at the bottom of the lift shaft with a broken neck, I would have had no-one to blame but myself. I should have read you the riot act after Martingy about not going one inch outside your instructions. Initiative is for those who've had the training and the briefing, not for amateurs.'

Her head drooped, a picture of misery. She took the letters from her dress pocket and handed them over.

'Two?' There was displeasure in his voice.

'I thought it looked important.'

He snorted, examined it; then stiffened, held it up to the light. That wasn't enough, so he switched on the desk lamp and held the envelope directly over the bulb.

'Code groups. My God. How did you spot them?'

'It was the weight of the paper inside. Or lack of it. It had to be something much lighter than ordinary paper, or even a cheque…'

She tailed off. His face was set, as if he were still angry. But then it changed to a look of exasperated affection.

'Clemency, if you were one of my agents, I'd be delighted with tonight. But you're not. You work for the Embassy. If anything had happened to you, even if it was just that they'd called the police, it would have been a disaster. A true diplomatic incident.'

'I suppose so.'

'And that wouldn't have been fair on you. You'd have been recalled to London, and perhaps never given another overseas posting, and all because of me.'

'Yes, but what you do is important, isn't it?'

He frowned.

'I think so,' he said slowly. 'It may not feel this way to the people back home, but we're fighting a war with the Soviets. A kind of slow-motion, undeclared war. Only thing is, they take it a hundred times more seriously than we do. They spend their money on tanks and missiles and spies. We want washing machines and TVs.'

He fell silent, swilling his drink round his glass.

'Sometimes it feels to me like the run-up to the last war. A few unpopular voices in the wilderness. The Soviets are throwing huge resources into espionage, subversion, black propaganda and the rest. But we can fight back. We can uncover what they're up to, thwart their plans. I know it's out of fashion now, but it's about patriotism, isn't it? So yes, a long answer. It is important.'

'What can I do to help?'

'You've done enough. In fact, you've done far too much. That's my fault, not yours, but there are some basic rules in this game.'

He stood, took her glass for a refill.

'Do the Soviets play by the same rules?' she asked, looking up at him.

'No, but that's all the more reason to leave it to the professionals.'

'And patriotism? Is that just for the professionals too?'

'Look, I'd like to run a private army, but that isn't how these things work.'

'I rather thought that we won the last war because we didn't stick to the rules all the time. That wartime is when you should cut through the red tape. And we are at war, aren't we?' she added innocently. 'You just said so.'

He filled their glasses, handed hers back to her.

'You want to help? I'll talk to London. There may be another mission coming up where I need some cover. Nothing like tonight, though. Nothing... active.'

She tried not to show her delight; tried and failed.

'But even in private armies, you need to learn to follow orders,' he said sternly. 'Can you do that?'

'Yes.'

'Then I'd be delighted to have you on my team.'

She wanted to laugh; he was so serious, and yet it felt as if she were being sworn into the Girl Guides.

'There is one thing, Peter. Wouldn't it be better if I knew some of what's going on? It's not just curiosity, but if I'd known those men were killers I wouldn't have thought of going up there.'

It's a fair point. I'll tell you what tonight was about. You've heard of BECO SA, I'm sure.' He gave Clemency a doubtful sideways glance. 'Anyway, they are one of the leading speciality chemical firms in Europe and have particular expertise in the production of complex organic chemicals on a large scale.

'What we've been told is that they've created a new way of creating high-impact polymers that could reduce input costs by 30% and improve quality. That's obviously of huge interest to us. BECO is not big enough to really exploit something like this to the full. They have already started looking round for an industrial partner with the scale to pull this off and a team from ICI is due to fly out next week to begin negotiations.

'And now comes this rumour that someone else has the process and wants to sell it to the highest bidder.'

'How much is it worth?' Clemency asked.

'What would we pay for exclusive rights? £2 million. Give or take. Plus an ongoing royalty. It really is that big. And it's not just about the money. It's about our industrial strength. Export earnings. Balance of payments. If our firms can't make enough money, we can't keep up our armed forces. Already we're having to retrench. The Navy's being slashed, regiments disbanded, new aircraft projects axed. The Soviets don't just want the dollars. They want us on our knees economically, and then militarily.'

'So it's our patriotic duty.'

'If you like. Anyway, Da Silva is a Mexican lawyer who has a very lucrative sideline in dealing with this kind of information. He knows where to get it and who to sell it to, and he's very adroit at not upsetting anyone along the way, including the Swiss authorities. For the same reason – nothing to do with morality – I don't think he'd be keen on murder. But if he thought his position was under real threat, he wouldn't hesitate.

'If he'd known who you are, I don't think he'd have done anything to you. But dressed like that – and I suspect you'd have done the brave thing and kept on pretending you were a waitress called Maria – it's possible he might have done something stupid.'

Somehow, Peter saying it now, when he was no longer angry, gave it all the more force. She wanted to get out these clothes. They had the taint of death about them.

'I should go,' she said, standing. 'Thank you so much for the drink.'

He stood too. Suddenly, they were very close. Clemency had a moment to realise what was coming.

'There is one other thing, Clemency.' He drew her to him and kissed her. Before she knew it, his arms were round her and she was pressed against him. The feelings washing around inside her were more of pleasure than anger or alarm, though they were there too. Most of all, she felt so safe.

'I shouldn't have done that, should I?' he said after a while.

'No.'

'Again?'

'Perhaps.'

'Good. But not tonight,' he said, stepping back. 'It wouldn't be fair to you.'

Not knowing what to say, she fell back on her enigmatic smile.

'Look, I should get you home.'

'I can't go back like this,' she said, gesturing at her dress.

'Oh yes.' For a moment, he was embarrassed. 'Your stuff's over here. You can use my bedroom to change.'

She closed the door and undressed slowly, looking around her. It was very masculine, even austere, lacking in personal touches, and presumably kept tidy by a daily maid. The only clue to his mind was the book by the bed: Conrad.

A bachelor's bedroom. She wondered who else had been in here, and what they had done, and what she would have done if he had not announced so firmly that it was time for her to go. And maybe, she thought to herself, he did that because what he really wanted was for her to stay.

◊

Clemency opened the door to her flat, then froze. It was the smell of cocoa; the recollection that she had gone off from the club without thinking of Hester; that Hester was now here waiting up for her.

'Clem?'

'I'm so sorry I had to go off like that,' she called back. 'It was work.'

Hester was lying on the sofa, wrapped in a shawl, a book across her knees; and she looked at Clemency indulgently.

'If you say so.'

'It was! Honestly. A sudden flap.'

'I'll warm up your cocoa and you can tell me all about him.'

Clemency continued to protest; but Hester had only to reach out and brush some cobwebs from her hair to reduce her to silence.

◊

Later, gazing at the patterns the street light shone faintly onto the ceiling, and listening to the last trams screeching back to the depot, she tried to make sense of the evening; and most of all, how she had felt in Peter's flat. There were plenty of Peter Aspinals in her world, and usually she had no trouble keeping them at a proper distance. But she'd let him kiss her; and if he had led her to the bedroom, she would have gone willingly. Even now, the feeling still gnawed inside her.

Yet that feeling had really started in Da Silva's house. She'd climbed like a thief into his study; stolen the letters; experienced the fear of discovery, then escaped to the safety of Peter's car. And throughout, she'd been alive in a way she'd never felt before.

She'd once been to a magic show, and become fascinated by the assistant, the girl who stood so trustingly while the heavy knives slammed into the board around her; who would enter the cabinet and let the swords be inserted; and who was then led triumphantly to the front of the stage, glittering and desirable, sharing the applause of the audience. And Peter was the magician who could take her to that world; saw her in half and put her back together again.

Only then did she remember the boy in the jazz bar. Nice enough; but Peter held the keys to another world.

5

Richardsons was one of the better chophouses in the City, all brass mirrors and leather banquettes. It was just off Gracechurch Street, in the heart of the shipping quarter, and business worth millions changed hands over the grilled steaks and claret. No-one thought it odd if you spoke in undertones or broke off when the waiter came over. It was a bit of a stretch from Whitehall, but Swan found it met his needs admirably. He eased himself into one side of the booth, tugged down his waistcoat, glanced briefly at the menu and then ordered what he always had: two lamb chops, boiled potatoes, grilled tomatoes and a bottle of Médoc. He glanced incuriously round, his eyes missing nothing, then turned to Peter.

'What's new?'

He had been asking this question for ten years, to Peter's certain knowledge, during which time he had grown fatter, greyer, more disillusioned; and yet the core fire still burned. Peter was ready with his answer.

'Schmitt delivered again, and the two new boys have both started producing. I'm keeping in contact with my opposite number at DAP and they seem to think we're behaving ourselves. No obvious sign of the bears getting too curious. And the man I mentioned in my last telegram – that might come to something.'

'Good. And yet I sense a 'but'?'

'No big deals, and no sign of one on the horizon.'

'Yes, I was feeling the same. Not a criticism, you understand. It just feels a bit flat. What about the industrial side? Our clients are becoming quite insistent on that. Ashton – he's a Dep Sec at Trade, I don't know if you've come across him – he's taken to calling me. It's usually the day after the monthly balance of payments figures are published, so I suspect the hand of his minister in that. All the same…'

'It's the old problem. Too much industrial…' Peter considered and discarded the word espionage. '…er, research and we'll rapidly become unpopular with our hosts. They're all over the East Germans and Czechs because of it. The plastics thing was fine because it was a Swiss firm coming to us.'

'Yes.'

Swan paused as their meals arrived. The convention of discussing their work as if it were a business – clients, meetings, deals, sales – was fine for casual cover, but wasn't to be stretched too far. There was some fussing with Swan's mustard, and Peter wondered where Swan's convoluted thinking was leading them. He could imagine the pressure. Each day, the *Times* and the *FT* were running gloomy headlines about Britain's economic decline, its loss of export markets. The lifeboat of EEC membership had sailed off again, leaving the country treading water. You could see it on the streets of Bern, where Peugeots and BMWs were pushing aside Austins and Rovers, and even the traditional cloths and woollens were coming from Italy or Belgium, not Bolton or Huddersfield. And economic decline meant military and political decline.

Yet it had been Swan himself who had summed up Peter's brief on industrial espionage: you can trawl, but not hunt. If information came his way that was useful to Britain's captains of industry, he could collect it and send it back to London, to be discreetly channelled to

ICI, Vickers, GEC or Lucas. But he couldn't go after it. No targeting of Swiss industrialists for honey-traps with 'singers' or 'dancers' who were high in charms and low in morals. No bribes to disgruntled employees, overlooked and bitter and with blueprints and specifications passing through their hands. All that was strictly off limits. Otherwise the DAP, the Swiss equivalent of MI5, would make his life impossible, until he would have to be recalled and replaced.

'It sounds to me as if you might have a bit of spare capacity,' Swan pronounced, then speared a potato with great care, so it remained in a single piece, ready to be combined with a morsel of meat. 'There's a rather interesting proposal we've received. I'd like someone I trust, someone with the right experience, to see if it stands up.'

'Outside Switzerland?'

'Yes. For various reasons I won't burden you with, I don't think our local chaps are well-placed to lead on this. In fact, better if the whole thing is run from head office.'

'Where?'

'Bucharest.'

Peter paused for thought. Romania was firmly in the Soviet bloc. If you were caught, it wouldn't be a slapped wrist and a seat on the next BEA flight home. These people would torture you, and maybe follow up with a show trial, and thirty years in a gulag or a firing squad at dawn. That depended if they wanted to make an example of you or keep you as a bargaining chip. Even if, after a couple of years, they made an exchange, you'd come home broken in spirit, wrecked physically, and the Service would want nothing more to do with you. Yes, some settlement grant and a soft job in a friendly firm. But his current life would be over.

There'd be no diplomatic protection, either, if he went in from 'head office', as Swan breezily put it.

But the other half of him was intrigued. There was the challenge of it. And he was flattered that Swan was thinking of him.

'What kind of job is it?'

'We've been asked to send a representative to neutral ground to hear a proposal and see if we can find a satisfactory means to import what they have to offer. It's a physical product. Each unit about the size of a side-plate. Not heavy, but fragile.'

'So it could go by air?'

'Yes, or be carried by an individual. There wouldn't be more than one or two such items in each shipment. The money, conveniently, would be paid via Switzerland.'

'Who are the principles?'

'That's the interesting thing. As far as we can make out, there's a connection to the Securitate. Of course, my first thought was whether this was some kind of trap. But I can't quite see how it works.'

Even though it would be his head on the block, Peter tended to agree. Secret services did maintain contacts with each other, even through the Iron Curtain.

'You know I know nothing about Romania?' he said casually.

'I wouldn't worry. You may not even need to go there.'

'Where's the meeting?'

'Paris. The weekend after next.'

They went into the arrangements. Peter mentioned in passing that he would need some cover if he were hanging around in Paris for the weekend.

'I can't provide anyone,' Swan said. 'What about the girl you took to Vienna? That went smoothly enough.'

'I'm not sure she's quite right for this one. I was thinking of one of the other clerks. I mentioned her in the last report.'

'Yes, I called up her file. She's awfully young.'

'She did a good job in Martigny.'

'Chasing a Moscow hood through the middle of the town? Not exactly by the book.'

'She got the film back. Yes, you'll say beginner's luck, but why not ride that luck a bit longer?'

Swan gave him a knowing look.

'So long as luck's the only thing to get ridden, eh?'

◊

Peter returned from England with him a nasty cold that needed several early nights with hot whiskey to get over. It was not until the beginning of the following week that he could find the time to take Clemency out to a discreet dinner somewhere far away from the haunts of his Soviet bloc opponents or, more importantly, the wagging tongues of the British community.

He gunned the engine of his MG – it made a particularly satisfying, throaty booming sound in the underground car park – and then sped up the ramp into the twilight. It should be a pleasant evening, and he was bringing her news of a trip to Paris – a far better present than flowers or a box of chocolates.

He was a little early, and as expected she wasn't ready, and so she invited him up, just as he hoped she would do. He liked to know as much as he could about those he worked with – in the most extreme circumstances, his life could depend on it – and he found her so hard to read. She was clearly highly intelligent, but hardly ever seemed to use her brain, and instead let it be filled with films and clothes and hairstyles. After the business with the letters, he had no doubts about her courage, even if like so many young officers he had known in SOE during the war it was based largely on a false belief in her own immortality. Loyalty? She would have the deep-grained sense of duty of her class – except that sometimes she came out with the most extraordinary cynical comments about politicians, the military, businessmen, or what she liked to call the Establishment.

'Help yourself to a drink,' she called from the bedroom.

He scouted around and found the remnants of a bottle of gin but no tonic water, and a half-bottle of dubious brown sherry. At least she wasn't a drinker. He settled for a glass of red wine from an opened bottle. It was surprisingly good.

He was used to taking in rooms at a glance, picking out the salient features, the ones that revealed character. Here, the problem was that there was too much raw material. The flat was cluttered with books and magazines, clothes and bags, towels and underwear drying on a clothes horse, too many cushions, too many wine bottles with candles stuck in them. Also, it was hard to separate Clemency's personality from that of her flatmate. Which of them owned the record player by the window and the pile of jazz records beside it? Who had chosen the poster of Elvis Presley in *GI Blues* on the wall by the kitchenette?

Everywhere were signs of a butterfly mind. A paperback splayed face-down on the arm of the sofa rather than put to one side with a bookmark inside. Unopened letters propped up against a vase of wilting flowers. A shopping list discarded on the sideboard, the pencil poised to roll onto the floor and break.

He'd once dated a dancer – not for long, and a long time ago – and she had lived a little like this, with everything thrown to one side until it was needed again. He'd found it charming, and then exasperating. He'd once made some comment about the chaotic scenes backstage. How could she live like that and then come on so calmly and perform? She'd laughed, but when he'd pressed her on it, she'd simply said that every woman lived like that: so much time on preparation, often in a rush, to be ready to go out; and then the serene face presented to the world.

Clemency emerged a little shyly. She had obviously gone to some trouble, though to Peter it was hard to see the difference, as she still looked like an art student. But if anything, that lack of sophistication, that youthfulness, made her more attractive. The only risk was that, if they did have an *affaire,* how serious she might become, and how awkward that might be. It wasn't arrogance; more the sense she was ready to fall for someone deeply.

'How was London?' she asked, as they set off into the night.

'Wet. But I have some news for you.'

Though he'd meant to keep back Paris until they were at the restaurant, it was too tempting to play the Fairy Godfather.

But her reaction was not at all what he expected.

'Me? Wouldn't it be better to go with someone who knows what they're doing?'

'I thought you'd be pleased.'

'I am. It was just a surprise.'

They fell silent, Peter ostensibly concentrating on the narrow lane that climbed into the hills from the main road. Joy wouldn't have been such a disappointment. She'd have given him a kiss or rested her hand on his knee; would have said how clever he was to arrange it; would have plunged at once into pleasurable planning about which restaurants they would visit, which hotels the FO travel allowances would stretch to.

He took his foot off the accelerator. Maybe he was being unfair. He wanted an assistant who would keep her mind on the job – and when she did so, he was annoyed with her.

They pulled up outside the restaurant. Typically, she got out of the car herself, not waiting for him to come around and open the door for her. Of course, you could argue that etiquette of this kind was outdated; but to him it had a charm and a purpose, and what did she propose to put in its place?

She turned to him.

'Peter, I'm sorry. It's not that I don't want to go to Paris with you. I do. But I don't think I should. Like I said, you need a professional with you.'

She was so sincere that the remains of his anger melted away.

'Don't start getting anxious on my behalf. This is purely routine. A milk run.'

'You said that about Martigny.'

'You did well.'

'I could have been killed. I could have got you killed.'

She was so serious, her eyes wide in the darkness, he didn't know whether to laugh or to pull her to him and kiss her, and not give a damn to where that would end up. Instead, he put his arm through hers and led her towards the restaurant.

'Cheer up. I know what to do. The Office would never countenance any official training. But an old friend of mine could help out.'

'Who is he?'

'*She* was with SOE during the war. Now she's the private secretary to the director of one of the top private banks in Zurich. She probably knowns more secrets than the rest of us put together. I'm sure she'd give you a bit of an introduction into our world. How to know if someone is following you, basic security, self-defence, that kind of thing. Would that help?'

'Yes, it would. Thank you.'

'That's my girl.' He patted her bottom. 'Come on. Let's feed.'

6

Clemency was alone in a coffee shop in the business district, wondering how a trained agent like Peter could have given her such a poor description of the woman she was to meet. Tall, dark, and in her forties, he'd said. It wasn't much to go on, but as it turned out, it was enough. Exactly on eleven, a woman entered and looked around confidently, picked Clemency out and came over to her table.

'Miss White?' She slipped off her cream doeskin glove and offered Clemency her hand. 'I'm Lucinda Jensen. May I?'

She was poised, sophisticated, her blue-black hair massed in a chignon to accentuate her neck, her coat and skirt in a deep blue plaid that brought out her eyes and might have been by Dior. Clemency at once felt gauche and shabby.

A waiter had appeared to pull out her chair, settle her in, and take her order. Perhaps she was a regular, or just had the air that the staff would recognise and respect. Working for the director of a Swiss bank would give you that authority; or you got the job because you already had it.

'So you're Peter's girl.'

'That sounds awful,' Clemency said, trying not to blush. 'I help him out from time to time. I work at the Embassy, you see, and —'

'No need to explain,' she said. 'It's how Peter likes to do things. But you're quite safe. He won't make you do things you don't want to. Or at least, he didn't to me. So how can I help?'

Clemency paused. In laying out her cards about her own past, and showing she understood the tentative state of Clemency's relationship with Peter, Lucinda had covered in less than a minute what would have taken Clemency all day to reveal. But in a way, it was a relief. At last, there was someone she could open up to. She tried to be just as direct.

'What Peter does is important. My part doesn't matter in comparison. I understand that. Except that if I muck something up, it could ruin everything. He really should have someone properly trained.'

'What you're asking for is a course lasting for months.'

Lucinda broke off while the waiter brought her pot of coffee and a plate of small, dry biscuits. She sniffed the coffee and nodded to show it passed.

'What is it that you and he are doing? I don't want to know any of the details. Just the technical side. Are you meeting a contact, picking up a package, surveillance?'

'It's been pick-ups so far.'

'And you're providing him with some cover.' Clearly this was all familiar to her. 'Will you be taking it somewhere on your own? As a courier?'

'No.'

She nodded. 'That would be more complicated. It needs a lot of tradecraft, as they call it these days. How to cover your own tracks and spot watchers and traps. But if it's just being with him, then it's more a state of mind than anything else. Have you worked out what your story is?'

'How do you mean?'

'It's fine to say you're with him for cover for him, but what about you? Who are you? What's your relationship to him? How do you feel about him? That has to be right, or you'll draw attention to you both. Are you in love with him? I mean, is that the idea? Are you supposed to be having an *affaire?*'

'Er... I suppose so. The contact is in Paris. We're going together.'

She was blushing now, but Lucinda was only amused.

'Such things happen,' she said dryly. 'And do you... no, let me put this another way. Do you find it hard to give the impression that you're in love with him?'

'I think I can do that.'

'Then that's fine. You have your cover. Next, can you obey orders? Even if he's being an absolute fool, he's in command. If he asks what you think, you can tell him. If you are sure he's about to make the biggest blunder in the world, you can tell him once, if there's time. But after that, just jump. Can you do that?'

'Yes.'

'Good.' She took a biscuit. 'That's all you need to know. But I can teach you more if you like. It can never do any harm.'

'Yes please. Even if it doesn't come in useful, it would help my confidence. Peter's taking me to the shooting range. I'm not going to be carrying a gun, but I think it will still help.'

'Guns are overrated,' Lucinda said definitely. 'You'd be better off learning self-defence. That way, if someone comes at you with a knife, or tries to grab you, you can get away.'

'I'd like to do that,' Clemency said eagerly, thinking back to Martigny. 'Do you know anyone who teaches all that?'

'I don't suppose there's a lot of call for that in Bern.

I can show you if you like. It's just some basic holds and falls. And we'll do a run through the town, to see how easily you can shake off a tail. How to spot if you've got one. That kind of thing. We'll see how much of it I can remember.'

She fell silent, a slight smile on her lips.

'Actually, it will be rather fun.'

◊

For two hours, Clemency had drawn a trail through the city. She had visited the cathedral, staring moonstruck up at the vaulted ceiling while checking to see if anyone was following. She had used a changing room in a department store to swop her sweater and hide her fair hair under a woollen cap, then slipped out of the rear entrance. She had jumped on a tram at the last moment, making sure no-one could follow. Now she was only a few minutes from her final destination: the Zytglogge, the medieval clock tower in the heart of the old town. It stood at the end of Gerechtigkeitsstrasse, which had colonnades along both sides, where you could dodge behind the heavy grey pillars, looking in shop windows, double back on yourself when you decided on a whim to return and gaze longingly at the fur tippet in the window of Schmidt's for just a few minutes longer.

She checked her watch. Five to four. She was looking forward to the tea and cake that Lucinda had promised. It would also be a relief to sit down for a while. She'd spent three hours that morning learning the basics of what Lucinda called *ju-jitsu* and she was bruised all over. It had been a little like a dance class, with the two of them dressed in black leotards and headbands: except that it had consisted of being thrown backwards onto a thin mat, or having her arm twisted half-out of its socket, or finding her feet swept away from her and ending up face down with Lucinda's knee in her back. Before they had started, she had been worried she might hurt the older woman. By the end, she was flushed and gasping, while Lucinda was hardly breaking sweat.

The Saturday crowds were thinning out. She looked up at the huge golden face of the Zytglogge, the red and yellow jester starting the carillon, the little parade of bears, followed by the heavy beat of the main bell high above.

Then she felt something poking into the base of her spine.

'Bang.'

Clemency swung around in exasperation.

'How did you find me?'

'I almost didn't,' Lucinda replied, looking very pleased with herself. 'In future, if you take a tram to shake off a trail, don't stay on the same street after you get off. I was on the next tram along and saw you out of the window. Now, I think you owe me tea.'

That was the wager that Clemency had been convinced she was about to win, but she held no grudge. Once she had eaten the rich cream cake she had certainly earned, and after her efforts had been dissected, and her morale restored with some praise for her as a promising pupil, she asked Lucinda about how she knew Peter.

'We met at Beaulieu,' she replied, a little wistful, quite different from her usual brisk and no-nonsense tone. 'Down on the Solent. The usual thing – a country house turned into a top-secret training school. We were both on some course or other. About blowing things up, I think. We were all terribly young, of course. It doesn't surprise me he stayed in after the war. He did have a lot of tenacity, and that's what you need in peace-time. It would have driven me mad.'

'Really?'

'Not, not really. I'd have loved it, or at least part of it. And occasionally I do miss it all. Peter and I kept in touch over the years. Of course, I don't know much about his work since then. I can imagine, but he doesn't tell me and I don't ask. I've helped him out a few times. I've made my life in Bern, and I would never do anything that the Swiss wouldn't like. But I happen to agree with what you said the other day: what Peter does matters.'

'I still worry that I won't know what to do.'

The older woman leaned forward, her voice lowered.

'When I volunteered, I was a little like you. This kind of work sounded important, and more interesting than cyphers. I had the training, and some of the other girls were weeded out at that stage, so I suppose they thought I'd be all right. But I had no more idea if I could cope than you do now, until I was parachuted into France.'

'But if I did lose my nerve? It could happen, couldn't it?'

'Oh, it does.'

For a while, she was lost in thought. When she spoke again, her tone was quite changed.

'In the third week I was in France, I went with my leader to check on one of the arms dumps, to see the explosives and so on were being stored correctly. He was a lieutenant in the Royal Engineers and was very hot on all that. The dump was in an old barn up in the hills above Montauban. Then some men from the *Milice* – the Vichy militia – turned up. It was probably a tip-off. There were always old scores being settled in the Resistance. There we were, looking through a hole in the door of the barn, and there were the three men, each one armed, walking towards us. And my leader froze. He had his gun in his hands, but he couldn't do anything.'

'Why?'

'I don't know. It happens. People talk about humans being essentially violent animals. I'm not so sure. The instinct not to kill is very strong, at least in most of us. And it wasn't about morality or chivalry. Another minute, and those men would have killed us; or captured us, which would have come to the same thing. I like to think I was tough back then, but I wouldn't have survived Ravensbrück.'

'What did you do?'

'I took the gun from him and shot them dead. And I was fine. That's how I knew I could do the work. I got my leader moving again and we took them away in their car and disposed of them in an abandoned quarry. We contacted the Resistance and got the arms moved. That was the end of it.'

Clemency had so many questions, but none that she dared ask. But after a moment, Lucinda picked up the story again, as if the memories she had dredged up were now leading her on.

'He never spoke about it. But he could never look me in the eye.'

She carefully poured herself some more tea, as if determined there should be no tremor in her hand, no spilt drop to ruin her composure.

'He was killed a week or so later. He was planting some explosives to bring down the mouth of a railway tunnel and it went off prematurely. I've always wondered about that. A different kind of courage, perhaps.'

And then the moment of openness, of vulnerability, was gone; as if she were frightened that Clemency might show her compassion.

'Anyway, that was all a long time ago. What matters is for you to learn the trade. Same time tomorrow?'

7

Their hotel was in the business district around the Bourse, and to Clemency it managed to be both seedy and stuffy. Then the restaurant Peter chose had dull food and awful service, and she'd known it would from the moment they stepped inside, because almost every table was empty. She'd been hoping they'd go on to the jazz club in the Rue de la Huchette, but when she suggested it, he just looked annoyed and said they weren't in Paris for fun. So they went back to the hotel, had a last awkward drink in the bar, and called it a night.

When they met again over breakfast, Peter's mood had brightened. He'd received a telephone message telling them to be at the Café de la Marmaton on Rue de la Fayette at 10am and await a call for a Monsieur Paul.

'It'll be the usual thing,' he said confidently, tearing at a croissant. 'They'll send us on a route round Paris so they can check we're not being tailed – either by our own people or by the opposition – and then they'll make the contact when they're ready. Put on some stout shoes because it could be a long day.'

She felt a little guilty for having cursed him to herself so roundly the night before. He was the one responsible for making this work, for assessing the risks and making sure the rendezvous went ahead. She was really just there for the ride. Sulking because she hadn't had the evening she was planning was just childish.

Back in her room, she put aside the clothes she'd planned to wear and went with something plain and sensible; and wrapped the new pair of flats she had bought in London back up in tissue paper. Then she checked herself in the mirror. With her short cream macintosh, and a little more eye-liner than usual, she looked the part of a Parisian secretary. She hurried down to where Peter was waiting in the lobby.

They walked to the café and lingered over coffees until the patron called the name of Monsieur Paul. Peter went off to the back, where the phone lived, and returned a few minutes later.

'We take Line 11 to République, then come back out and walk to Oberkampf. Then we take the line to Jaurés and switch to Line 2 towards Porte Dauphine. We go into the Bois de Boulogne to the café by the children's playground and that's where they make the contact.'

They hurried through a shower of rain and plunged into the nearby métro station. There, everything was as Clemency remembered: the passages lined in white tiles; the smell of stale cigarette smoke and sweat; the platforms with the tracks, slightly menacing, leading off into the wide, flat tunnels to each side. She had always avoided the métro when she could; it was too smelly and noisy, and she much preferred walking. At least the train wasn't crowded.

'How long were you posted here for?' Peter asked as they pulled into the tunnel.

'Ten weeks. I had a room in a flat on the Rue de l'Université. It's in the seventh, so I could just walk over the Pont de la Concorde and past the Tuileries. Not a bad way to get to work, was it?'

She realised that her way of referring to the arrondissements of Paris by their numbers – the seventh, or the second – irritated him; as if she were trying to prove she knew Paris better than he did. But when they emerged at the Place de la République, it was she who knew the way and led him down the Avenue de l'Armée to Oberkampf station.

'By the way,' he said, 'don't start trying to be a super-spy and seeing if we're being tailed. That's not for us to worry about. The whole point is for us to look innocent.'

His tone was slightly crushing and they walked on in silence. Usually, she chatted on about everything and nothing when they were together, and after a while the quiet began to worry her, as if she were trying to make him apologise. But she couldn't think of anything to say.

'Oh, by the way,' he said. 'I asked the Office about overtime, and I'm afraid they won't pay it. You see, you're not attached to the Service, so they can't authorise it; and obviously you can't claim it from the Embassy, because then it would show you weren't on holiday.'

'I suppose so.'

'I've asked about a discretionary payment, but I wouldn't pin any hopes on it. Anyway, you don't need the money for anything in particular, do you?'

'Please don't worry. I'm sorry I mentioned it.'

They walked down the stairs into the métro, bought their tickets and took their places on the platform, all without speaking. The train came, the warning klaxon blared and the doors slammed shut, so much more aggressive than on the tube. Peter took out a newspaper and began to read the business pages.

Clemency's mind went back to the previous evening, when the three of them had met for a drink, to say thank you to Lucinda and let her wish them well for their mission. And since that evening, everything with Peter had gone wrong.

It had started with Peter's amused and slightly patronising attitude to her training. Lucinda had suggested a demonstration, and Clemency had managed to disarm him when he had come at her with a butter knife. She hadn't hidden her delight, and that had put him in a bad mood. Perhaps in revenge, he'd made a point of flirting with Lucinda, and Clemency had discovered just how jealous she could be. And as they'd exchanged memories of their wartime training over dinner, she'd felt left-out and ignored, like a bored child.

But the evening had unsettled Clemency more profoundly that that. She had never met anyone quite like Lucinda. She lived alone but gave no sign of regretting it. Her life had work, friends, interests, and apparently no gap the size of a husband, let alone two or three children. She had all the poise and sophistication that Clemency lacked. Her flat was in the old town, with one huge living room, beautifully furnished with Scandinavian furniture, lots of vibrant colours, a pine floor that scented the whole flat, a balcony that looked out over the park and the river.

As much as she felt jealous of Lucinda, she envied her.

◊

They emerged from Porte Dauphine station onto Avenue Foch. Two rows of grand, dull buildings stretched away to the distant block of the Arc de Triomphe, and these were so far apart that there was space for a wide strip of grass and trees, almost a park, along each side of the road. In the other direction, it was a vast building site, with red and white striped barriers guiding the traffic between mechanical excavators, piles of bags of cement and steel supports, pits and mounds of dirt and rubble. There was the taste of dust in the air and the noise of drills and pile-drivers, diesel engines and cement-mixers, was relentless.

'What the hell are they building?' Peter's question was rhetorical, but as it happened, Clemency knew the answer.

'The *Périphérique*.'

'What's that?'

'A kind of motorway that's going to go all the way around the city. Three lanes each way.'

'Good God.'

There were crossings marked *Piétons* and they picked their way through the barriers, towards the distant trees on the edge of the Bois de Boulogne. There were no other pedestrians in sight, and Clemency saw that the directions they had been given were not as random as they had seemed; it would be difficult to be followed on foot, and impossible by car.

Even inside the Bois there were more excavations, diversions, noise and even the sound of a chainsaw attacking one of the noble oaks.

'I can't believe they're doing this to Paris,' Peter said.

'It's not a museum,' Clemency said. 'People have to live and work here.'

He grunted; once they had left the works behind, his mood lifted a little, but he couldn't leave the subject alone.

'It's the same in London,' he complained. 'These urban motorways they're planning to build. Everyone wants to drive everywhere. It's preposterous.'

'You have a car.'

'That's different. I work hard and I can afford it. But you have these kids of twenty working in a factory, thinking they're entitled to their own car, and before you know it, they're on strike for more wages.'

His assurance was putting her teeth on edge.

'I want a car,' she said, knowing it would rile him. 'Why shouldn't I have one?'

'But how on earth could you afford one?'

'I'm saving up. My overtime, mainly.'

He ignored that.

'Surely the point of Paris is you don't need a car,' he said. 'There's the métro.'

'I'd rather drive if I could.'

'I grant you the métro can be a bit crowded at times, but—'

'Maybe if you had your bottom pinched ten times a day you'd think differently.'

'Well, you shouldn't wear your dresses so short. It's just asking for it.'

'This isn't short. In London, they're up to here.' She hitched up her skirt to show him and was delighted by his appalled reaction.

'For God's sake, Clemency. This might be Paris, but even so. Anyway, what car do you have your eye on?'

'A Mini,' she replied without a moment's hesitation. 'In Iris Blue. Or Surf Blue. I can't decide.'

'How much will that set you back?'

'Four hundred and thirteen pounds, ten shillings and sixpence.'

'Really? You could get a lot more car for your money. A second-hand Morris Minor, maybe, or—'

'But the Mini is such fun,' she protested. 'I know it's a bit basic, but you can zip around in it and park it anywhere and it's so clever how much space there is inside. And there are all these places where you can stow things away. They even have these wicker baskets that go under the seats. Oh, you're laughing at me now.'

But she didn't mind. That condescending, indulgent look was better than distant disapproval.

'I just can't see why you need one.'

He sounded just like her father, when she'd told him of his plan. But there was nothing in the world she wanted more. If she went to a club in London, she wouldn't be depending on one of the boys to give her a lift home or have to wait for a bus in the rain. When she went to stay with her parents, she could head off in the evening to see one of her old school friends, and not be stuck in the rambling old house with her parents' disapproval every night. It wasn't that she didn't love them, but she didn't want to be trapped there. The Mini was like a magical flying carpet, and cheap at the price. Another six months, with her overseas allowances, and she'd have the money.

They came to the café and found a table under the trees. There were children playing on the swings and slides and roundabouts, all smartly dressed and watched over by the mothers, each impossibly glamorous. Peter ordered coffees in his awful French, took out his cigarette case and offered it to her.

'No, thanks. That's one of my economies. Think what you save, not smoking for a year. I worked out I was spending four shillings a day on them.'

'Well at least you aren't one of those awful types who saves on cigarettes by cadging them off other people.'

She watched him light up, take a deep draught and exhale high into the air. The thin blue smoke began to drift away in the faint breeze. Strange how it was here at the café, where the exchange was due to be made – so presumably the moment of greatest risk – that he became so relaxed.

'I still can't believe you'd spend all that on a car. There could be other things you'd buy first. A television, perhaps.'

'If you live in the provinces, then perhaps. But in a city, why do you need television? You have everything for real. Theatre, films, ballet. Something new every night. Why be on your own and have the worst seat in the house?'

'Well, I agree with you there.'

'What do you spend your money on?' she asked, encouraged by the return of his good humour. 'What's your secret vice?'

He laughed.

'I do spend a bit too much on fishing gear. And the MG takes a bit of looking after, especially out here. The Swiss may think they know about precision engineering, but it takes them an age to get the old girl right again.'

'It's worth it, though. It's a lovely car. Do you do much touring?'

'Oh yes. One of the perks of the job. I've been down to Barcelona in her, and into Italy, Bavaria, Austria. There's no better way to travel.'

'I've never been to Italy.'

'Really? We should do something about that. It's only three hours to the border from Bern. After that, you can make pretty good time on their roads. They're not quite up to Autobahn standards but still fast enough.'

They chatted on, and Clemency was surprised by his interest in the art and culture of Italy, so that he could talk knowledgably and with enthusiasm about what she must see in Florence, Verona, Sienna. For once, there was no hint of condescension as he told her the best cafes, restaurants, hotels. The conversation was also a kind of mutual apology, a way of putting behind them the tensions and misunderstandings of the last two days. Before they knew it, the waiter was hovering meaningfully. Peter ordered more coffees.

'Good God. We've been here an hour.'

'Have we?' She was surprised by his tone, until she remembered why they were there. Meanwhile he was back in his professional role, leaning back in his chair so he could scan around him.

'What's the problem, do you think?' she asked.

'The most likely explanation is that we do have a tail.'

'A nanny, maybe?' she said. There were two or three nannies or governesses or whatever, dressed in their informal uniform of black or grey. Only after she'd said it did she realise how absurd it was.

'Our best bet to head back to the hotel,' Peter decided. 'We'll go slowly, in case they find a chance to make the drop. The problem is, if we try and lose the tail – assuming there is one – we could lose our contact as well.'

'Perhaps they could have just posted it to us. Or dropped it off at the Embassy.'

'Not so good for us if they had,' he said lightly. 'No trip to Paris.'

They retraced their steps, Clemency painfully aware of how easy it would be for them to be followed by the KGB or the GRU. Any of the passers-by might be watching them, reporting back to nearby cars, and then perhaps from there by radio to some central command post, perhaps in the Soviet Embassy, where their moves might be plotted on a board.

And might they go further than just watching? As they threaded their way through the construction site by the Porte Dauphine, the mechanical excavators and cranes and bulldozers took on sinister form. With all this teeming activity, it would be so easy for there to be an accident – a load of steel reinforcing rods slipping from their chains, or a truck running out of control – and they could be wiped out. Had something like that happened to the Romanian agent they were supposed to meet?

She didn't share her fears with Peter, but she stood close beside him as they waited on the métro platform, relieved that there were no other passengers nearby, who might step forward as the train approached and push her under its wheels.

She picked up a discarded paper to try and take her mind off her fears. Even the account of the border fighting between China and India, the war of words over Cuba, was a relief. Each time the train pulled into a station she looked up automatically to check where she was, and she glimpsed Peter face, set and watchful.

Back at the hotel, there was a message for Peter. He stood by the concierge desk for a long time, the paper in his hand, thinking furiously. She wished he'd talk to her, but knew that she mustn't be a distraction, that he was the one with the responsibility to the mission as well as to themselves.

He turned back to the desk clerk and explained that their plans had changed and they would have to leave at once. Clemency suggested she should go and pack while the man made up the bill; but Peter quietly told her to stay where she was. With a shiver, she realised he was thinking there might be a GRU agent waiting in their rooms.

Peter would clearly be far happier if he were on his own, and not worrying about how to get her to a place of safety. The risk might not be that great. There was no reason to think that, given they hadn't received the package, the GRU would do anything other than watch them. But could one be sure?

They went to the lift. As it rose to the fifth floor, he

spoke to her quietly.

'I want you out of Paris. We'll pack up and get you on a train at Gare de l'Est. Then I'm going to fly back to London from Orly and report in. OK?'

They took a taxi to the station, then passed through to the main concourse where enamelled plates showing the destination of each train hung from a gantry. Her heart sank when she saw that the next train to Bern was not until 23h05. She could hardly ask Peter to stay with her for all those hours; but she was alarmed at the idea of waiting there alone. She wanted to get away from Paris, and not only so Peter could fly to London. Any of the destinations on the boards would do: Nevers – Clermont – St Etienne; Lyon – Marseilles – Nice.

'Look, there's a train in ten minutes for Milan. It stops at Lausanne. I can get a connection from there.'

'Really?'

She had said it confidently, but she had no idea if it were true.

'Watch my case.' Before he could answer, she was running to the ticket office, weaving through the crowd. Mercifully the queue was short, but it gave Peter a chance to catch up just as she reached the window.

'A single to Lausanne.'

Peter leant past her.

'Première classe,' he said, then turned to her. 'Least I can do.' He began counting out the ten-franc notes for the women behind the window. 'I was planning to take you out for a rather good dinner, so I'm still ahead of the game.'

'That would have been nice,' she said absently, as she peered around to find platform nine.

'Another time, maybe.'

She missed the regret in his voice; but once they had

found an empty compartment, and he had stowed her case and coat on the overhead rack, and checked she still had her ticket, she realised there was something she should say.

'Peter, I'm sorry this has all gone wrong. And that I've been such bad company. I'd understand if you didn't ask me to work with you again. There'd be no hard feelings.'

'Yes, there would,' he said. 'My feelings. We're a team, aren't we? Now make sure you have a good dinner and I hope you make that connection.'

He turned to go; then stopped in the doorway and turned back again and kissed her. Outside the guard was calling out that the train was ready to depart, but he ignored it.

'You should go,' she said with a smile.

'I just thought you needed a souvenir of Paris.'

Then he was gone. She lowered the window in time to see him step down from the carriage door just as the guard climbed up, whistling as he did so. The train jerked and began to move. Peter walked alongside; a proper romantic send-off, just like in the films.

'Be good. I'll see you on Tuesday.'

'Have a safe flight.'

She wanted to say more; wanted him to say more, too; but even so, maybe Paris hadn't been so bad.

◊

She was too drained to think of reading; just sat gazing out of the window as the dark countryside rolled by. Mainly she thought of Peter; telling herself he would be on the plane from Orly by now, and quite safe; missing him, too.

Her train was delayed near Dijon and sheb had to wait in Lausanne for the same train she could have caught all the way from Paris. But she got a space in a couchette and managed a few hours sleep before being decanted into Bern's main station at half past nine the next morning, and from there it was a tram and a walk and then at last she was climbing the familiar stairs to her own flat.

She dumped her suitcase, handbag and coat. It was odd being home during the day, alone in the flat with Hannah at work. She yawned. Should she make herself coffee, or try and sleep?

She began to unpack her suitcase. The contents mocked her: the dress she had planned to wear to dinner; the silver necklace; the best, most insubstantial underwear, just in case things got out of hand.

And beneath everything, a book in French, but by a Romanian poet.

She had never seen it before in her life, and as she picked it up, a bookmark fluttered to the floor. On it, in pencil, was a Paris telephone number. The Romanians must have gone into her hotel room in Paris and left it for her to find.

There was no phone in the flat, so she hurried down to the café on the corner and called the switchboard at the Embassy.

'I need to pass a message on to Major Aspinal,' she said. 'It's rather urgent.'

It turned out he'd left a message for her to call him on a London number before she did anything else. She fretted as she waited to be connected.

'Clemency?' Peter's voice was tense.

'Are you all right?'

'Yes, fine,' he said dismissively. 'But I need you to

do something for me. Go and wait in your flat. Don't open the door to anyone. Pack a bag. A man called Franz Toller will come and pick you up in an hour. You're going to stay in a hotel for a couple of days.'

'What? Why? And who is Franz Toller?'

'He's a former policeman. Now he's a private detective. He does some bodyguard work for me from time to time.'

It was all making less and less sense.

'Peter, what's going on? Why do I need a bodyguard?'

'You know the favour you did for me? When you were a waitress?'

She thought of the night, the climb up to the study, the mix of fear and the excitement that was better than anything. Then she remembered Peter's warning about the man's ruthlessness.

'Does he know it was me?'

'Not exactly. But... look, it might not be connected. But the girl Maria who was going to do it – the one who cried off – she's been found dead. In an alley. A knife in the ribs.'

8

For Peter, the next day was slow torture. He wanted to be back in Bern, sorting out the mess. It wasn't only the danger to Clemency. There was his man on the inside of Da Silva's organisation, and Herr Ruppel, and even the boy with the measles who, like Maria, had failed to turn up. But he had an early-morning meeting with Swan, to be followed by a day of briefing. If he were lucky, he could make the last flight back to Switzerland. But he couldn't cry off, because that would lead to explanations about the operation against Da Silva that he really didn't want to have to answer.

All night he'd turned it over in his mind, and the most likely explanation was that Da Silva had somehow heard in advance about Maria's involvement in a plan to rob him, and had arranged for her to be bought off, or threatened, or both. She in turn had warned the boy.

But then Peter had gone ahead with the plan and so Da Silva, assuming that Maria had double-crossed him, had her liquidated. Da Silva was also sending Peter himself a signal to back off. In fact, he was at far greater risk than Clemency. There was no reason to think Da Silva even knew she existed.

Swan had already made contact with the Romanians through the Paris phone number. They had, in some unspecified way, come close to being exposed by counter-intelligence agents in Paris, and it would be safer to meet in Romania. If the British wanted to deal, they would have to send out a representative to Bucharest. If not, they made clear, there were always the Americans, or the French.

'You'll be going as a British businessman,' Swan told Peter. 'There's a firm called Lansing. They make handling equipment. One of the directors is an old friend and happy to help us out. You'll fly to Bucharest from London. The commercial attaché at our embassy will liaise with their Ministry of International Trade and set up a series of meetings for you with potential clients. Then you go on by train to Constanta. It's the main port, on the Black Sea coast. Lots of opportunities to sell your kit. More meetings. I expect that's where the contact will be made. Then back to Bucharest and fly back to London. Five days. And for all but an hour or two, you are the deputy European sales manager for Lansing, and your one interest in life is flogging fork-lift trucks.'

'OK.'

Another kind of chief might have made something of this: looked Peter in the eye and told him how important this was, or the good of the Service or even of the country. Swan just took it for granted that Peter would go. He told him to get a full briefing from the South-East Europe desk that afternoon, and into the next morning if necessary.

'When will this trip be?' Peter asked.

'Next week. Oh, and you'll need a secretary to go with you. The usual status thing, plus someone to let you focus on the job. She can hand you the right price list and make sure there are plenty of upbeat telegrams going back to your bosses at Lansing. Same girl as before?'

'I can ask her.' Perhaps Clemency would be safer

being away from Bern for a few days.

'Don't tell her anything, of course. You know what girls are like. There's always that one friend they have to confide in. And don't bother with any briefings or training. The more innocent of tradecraft she is, the better. Just get her to work on her cover story. If necessary, she can be new to Lansing and so doesn't know much about what they do anyway. That all right?'

Swan's casual briefing was in contrast to the hours of work Peter put in back at Broadway, and then with the Board of Trade and the Foreign Office. Some of what he learned gave him pause for thought. The Securitate was, for the size of the population, the largest intelligence agency in the Soviet bloc. As well as the usual external espionage networks, and the internal surveillance and counter-espionage departments, it ran prisons, a vast number of informers, and even had its own uniformed forces, 20,000 strong and heavily armed. It had been set up by the Russian NKVD and was brutal even by their standards.

But there was a theory that the Romanian leadership were tiring of such strong direction from Moscow. Nothing so dramatic as a breach; more a sense that Romanians should develop their own economy, and not just send raw materials to their Communist allies and receive a few poor-quality cars and radios in return. Peter had read back through the reporting telegrams from the British Legation in Bucharest and there was a clear thread of Romania asserting itself, whether in closer ties with the Chinese Communists or in ending the compulsory teaching of Russian in Romanian schools.

So maybe, the theory went, the Romanian secret

service was becoming more independent. That might be where this approach was coming from; and London wanted to understand it, perhaps even exploit it.

There was a risk; but there was always a risk. He only hoped that what the Romanians were selling was going to be worth it.

◊

Even after Clemency had read about the murder in the papers, it was hard to connect the woman's death to her own world. With Peter away, she turned to Lucinda, who provided the brisk reassurance that Clemency craved. Over tea in the café next to the hotel, she listened to Clemency's halting account and gave her firm opinion: this wasn't her fault, or Peter's – just a piece of rotten luck. The girl had known the risks, and if she had been warned off by Da Silva, she weas a fool not to confide in Peter.

'If he'd known, he'd have called off the operation. Then she'd have been in no danger. She was a little idiot to just not turn up like that.'

But though Lucinda was exasperated, there was compassion in her voice too.

'Peter said this was like a war,' Clemency said tentatively. 'I suppose that means obeying orders.'

'Exactly.' Then, as if that sounded too harsh, she added: 'I know you'll think about her. That's human nature. This is a much more personal war than one with tanks and planes. And Peter will be shaken up too, though he probably will try to hide it. You'll have to help him with that. The best thing you can do is to carry on and not be a worry to him.'

Lucinda tilted her head to study Clemency, her

eyes narrowed.

'You do want to carry on, don't you?'

'More than ever.'

◊

Once Peter had returned and reassured her that there was really very little risk, Clemency was more than happy to leave the hotel and go back to her flat and her ordinary life. She felt quite safe walking to and from the Embassy, putting the tradecraft Lucinda had taught her into practice: always taking a different route, at a different time, and keeping to busy streets and crowded places. The greatest danger was outside her own front door and she took to checking the cars in the street for anything out of place, like an unmarked van or a numberplate from a different canton.

The only other precaution was that Peter said they shouldn't be seen together in Bern.

'There's a chance Da Silva will come after me. If he does, he might see you as way to get at me.'

Like murder, kidnapping was something for the cinema at the weekend, not for her working life. And in the next few days, there was no time for anything but work. The head of chancery, Dansby-Gregg, was seriously displeased to be told that one of his clerks wanted a few days off at short notice and made sure she was loaded with extra shifts to make up for it. And coding was a nightmare when you were tired, because you made silly mistakes and had to start over again.

But the work was better than thinking about Da Silva and the dead girl Maria. She followed Lucinda's advice, and never mentioned her to Peter.

But she thought of her often, and of what her last moments would have been like, and sometimes it was Clemency herself who was pushed into an alley, who felt the blade of a knife slide between her ribs, and who was thrown aside on a pile of rubbish to take her last rasping breaths.

◊

Clemency had another lesson in the realities of her new world three days later. After her morning shift she visited the library of the British Council, hoping for something that would give her a smattering of Romanian before her mission began. They had an elderly English-Romanian dictionary and a solitary novel and thinking these were better than nothing took them to the librarian, Smithson, to borrow. He gave her a curious look from under his shaggy grey eyebrows.

'Planning a trip there?' His tone was sarcastic, though not hostile.

'No, just curiosity. Someone told me that if you have French, Romanian is easy to learn. I thought it might be helpful one day.'

'I wouldn't bother. It's a rotten place.'

His vehemence surprised her. She would have said that Smithson, though morose, and rather looked down on by the rest of the Legation – ineffectual, often drunk, and only useful for helping local companies stage the plays of Shaw and Shakespeare – was an easy-going man, comfortable in his semi-retirement. But she had clearly touched a nerve.

'Have you been?' she asked brightly.

'I was posted there, for all of six weeks. In Forty-seven.'

'What happened?' He clearly wanted to talk, and she was eager for any scraps of knowledge about the place.

'We set up an office for the British Council there. The usual. Library, lectures, started on a programme of cultural exchange. I thought it would be a plum posting. In some ways it's a beautiful city, Bucharest. But sad. Not just the war damage and the Communists taking over. They're a gloomy bunch, the Romanians. Fatalistic. Almost a death wish, some of them. You'll get that quick enough if you plough through that,' he added, tapping the novel sitting on the desk between them.

'So if a posting came up there, you don't think I should apply?'

'I'll tell you what happened, and then you make your mind up.' He glanced around, but as usual the library was almost empty. 'We took several Romanian nationals onto the staff. You know how it is. London like locally-engaged staff because they're cheaper, and you always need a few because they know how the place works. Anyway, we got set up, and then the Communists were all over the Legation with accusations of spy rings and the rest of it. Tit for tat expulsions. They pulled in a couple of the diplomats, even, and gave them a hard time before sending them home. Not actually imprisoning them, just being as nasty as they could.

'And they did it to our Romanian staff, too. Arrested the lot. They said we'd recruited them as spies. One of them was an artist, another a poet, there was a dancer and a couple of teachers. The thing was absurd. But the Communists wanted a show trial. And they closed the British Council office and I was sent home. And that was the end of my pleasant visit to Romania.'

'And they put them on trial? What happened then? Did we protest?'

'Oh, we protested. My diplomatic colleagues put in protest after protest, asking for them to be released. I hear they're still doing it.'

'You mean they're still in prison? But this was fifteen years ago.'

'Still in prison, all of them. Somehow our protests have not had the desired effect, though I'm sure we've done everything we can,' he added with a twist to his mouth. 'They weren't alone. There were a number of Romanian managers of British oil firms and when they were nationalised they put the managers in jail. They're still there too. And some others they said were spying. I don't think they shot any of them, but they were sent to do hard labour on the Danube Canal and some of them didn't survive.'

'That's terrible.'

He beckoned to her to lean over the desk. Unwilling but fascinated, she did so and smelt the alcohol on his breath, though it was only eleven in the morning.

'I shouldn't have seen it,' he breathed. 'But I have my sources. We're supposed to be friends of the Romanians now. Something about them sticking two fingers up at Moscow. Anyway, there's talk of reopening the British Council office there, and naturally our line has been that this can't happen until our people are out of jail. And do you know what they're saying in London?'

'No.'

'I saw the letter. They say the prime objective is better relations with the Romanians, and we shouldn't worry about the past. They say it's like being a general. You need to concentrate on the military objective and not worry if some of your troops are killed gaining it. What do you think of that?'

'It's awful.'

'Isn't it? They say that one of them was dying of a perforated ulcer in prison, and right to the end – he was delirious – he was shouting out, *Churchill knows about me, he has written a letter, I will be out of here tomorrow.* I tell you, I've got a year to go and then it's my pension and you won't see me for dust. I'm sick of the lot of them. There's no-one they wouldn't sell down the river.'

However much he repelled Clemency, with his rotten breath and his sense of failure and the bitterness that oozed like stale alcohol from every pore, she couldn't forget the story, or the man dying in a Romanian jail. Most of all, she couldn't forget Smithson's last words.

She trusted London. If she and Peter ran into trouble, they would do everything they must to get them out again. She had to believe it. But now she wondered just how hard they would try.

9

She peered through the window. The plane was still descending through thick clouds, and there was nothing to be seen, except for the glow of the navigation lights, blinking red. The sound of the engines had faded, and there was a hush in the cabin, as if others were starting to think that they should be on the ground by now, that the quiet wasn't right.

She glanced at Peter, but he was still deep in his newspaper. On the other side of the aisle, two businessmen were exchanging glances, and by the cockpit door, the dark-haired stewardess was gazing out into the clouds.

Then the nose of the plane rose sharply. The engines wound themselves urgently, the propellers biting at the air, lifting them up, forcing her back into her seat, drowning out some stifled cries of alarm from further back in the cabin.

'I thought so,' Peter said, folding his paper. 'They should have decided to go around way before this. It's too thick to land. We'll probably have to divert.'

She breathed out, relieved by Peter's calmness and by the seconds passing without the plane slamming into the ground.

'You knew they'd do that? You could have told me.'

'You seemed happy enough.'

The left wing dipped abruptly, and he leaned closer.

'You can never tell with an outfit like TAROM. Is the pilot good at flying, or just a good Communist? But I was watching the stewardess…'

'You surprise me.'

'…and she didn't look too flustered. So I guess we have an ex-Romanian air force man at the helm, and that's probably not a bad thing. Too confident, which is why he didn't divert. But quick reactions. It evens out.'

Peter returned to his paper with an air of infallibility. But in fact the pilot didn't divert, gave it another try, and a few minutes later they were screeching along the slick wet tarmac of Bucharest's airport.

The stewardess announced in a fluid, melodious language that Clemency assumed was Romanian, and then in excellent French, and then in very poor English, that they were welcome to Bucharest, the time was 16.47, there was light rain, no smoking until inside the terminal, and they were thanked for travelling with TAROM. One or two men around her were clutching packets of cigarettes disconsolately. Peter stood and passed her coat and handbag down from the rack.

'We'll get a taxi to the hotel, and then we're meeting the commercial attaché at eight.'

They filed off the plane, down the stairs and on to Romanian soil; or at least, concrete. Clemency looked about her, wondering if the Soviet Bloc should look different. But it was the same as any other airport; an expanse of dreary tarmac, some low hangars in the distance, and a bus waiting a few yards away, with the more heavily-built passengers pushing their way on to secure the few seats.

Inside the modern concrete and glass terminal, they queued up patiently while the border police made their interminable checks. Apart from the passports issued in their cover names – Peter had become Henry Fleming, the deputy sales manager for Lansing Bagnall Limited, and Clemency was Caroline Green, his secretary –

they were both 'clean', as Peter had put it in far-away London; no weapons, no miniature cameras, no high-denomination notes for bribery or corruption. If the customs men wanted to tear their bags apart, they would find nothing. And so, after less than an hour of standing in line, being scrutinised by hard-faced men in gaudy uniforms or ill-fitting blue suits, they were in a taxi and passing down one of the city's wide, tree-lined boulevards, and Clemency was beginning to think that maybe the claim to Bucharest as the Paris of the east was not as ridiculous as she had thought.

'When's the first meeting tomorrow?' Peter asked, easing into his role.

'You're having breakfast with the deputy purchasing manager of the national freight company. Then at 9am there'll be a car at the hotel to take us to ASTI SA. They're a steel distributor and are interested in our range of heavy-duty hoists. The main contact there is a Mr V. Danilescu. And we'll be accompanied by a Mr T. Illiescu from the Ministry of International Trade.'

She rattled through the rest of the day's programme, while Peter frowned out of the window at the passing apartment blocks, the yellow trams, the surprising number of parks.

The Cismigui Hotel was on yet another wide, tree-lined boulevard, and the outside was Parisian down to the grey stone and mansard roof. Inside, it was depressing, being cold, a little dirty and largely empty. Despite that, there was a long wait while the desk clerk took their passports away to be examined in a back room, and longer still until a porter came to take their bags.

Clemency's room was as large as her whole flat in Bern, all faded grandeur, down to the claw-footed bath with an inexhaustible supply of tepid water. But from the window there were incomprehensible signs, buses in unfamiliar livery, people who dressed or even simply looked different to those in London or even Paris or Bern. It was a genuinely foreign country, and that alone excited her, even when she forgot about why she was there.

Peter had warned her that their hotel rooms would be bugged, and that they would probably be followed, their bags might be searched, and she should never at any time discuss why they were there. In a genuine emergency, she should mention a fictional colleague at Lansing, John Standfast, and Peter would find a way in which they could safely communicate. But until contact was made, they would live and breathe fork-lift trucks and power hoists.

The man from the Embassy took the same line, and Clemency sat and listened at the bar while he chatted to Peter about the economic situation in Romania. She took some notes, more to keep awake than anything else, but she liked the piano music in the background, the sharp white wine and the bowl of salted almonds that the barman kept replenished. There were also people to look at: not many, and not easy to see, as the bar was naturally dark and the light bulbs were of a strange kind that hardly gave out any light, so that you could look straight at the filament glowing red at their centre. But she could wonder about the two men in suits sitting by the door and saying so little; the two women gossiping in low voices further along the bar, overdressed in the styles of a decade before; a group of Americans in sports jackets and crew cuts, tanned and muscled, talking in a desultory way about oil rigs and baseball. Or maybe it was the pianist, with his bony

skull and huge eyes and long spider-like fingers, who
was working for the Securitate.

And the commercial attaché droned on.

'Of course, everything here comes back to oil, in
terms of international trade. There's growing interest
in diverting more of this into petrochemicals, and I can
see some of the new factories they're building needing
your kind of kit. But most firms here have to take what
the Russians or East Germans offer them, and if there
is any foreign currency to be had, Linde have that just
about sewn up. Except for timber, where there's an
American firm called, what was it...'

'Hyster?' Peter offered, who had clearly done his
homework.

'That's them.'

'We don't really compete in that sector,' Peter
explained, and Clemency wondered whether the
commercial attaché knew why they were there, and this
was all an act for the Romanian intelligence service; or
if even the British Embassy was being kept in the dark.
Either way, it proved what Peter had claimed and that
she had not really believed – that espionage could be
surprisingly boring.

After ordering another round of drinks, Peter
excused himself and strolled confidently off to find the
toilets, with the two Romanians in suits, and the two
women at the bar, both watching him closely.

'This must be all very dull for you, Miss Green,' the
attaché said, with a faint, uninvolved smile.

'Not at all,' she replied, equally polite, though
amused inside to be actually addressed by her cover
name. 'This is my first trip to a Communist country
and I'm finding it very interesting.'

'You probably know that it's a very bad idea to talk

to any Romanians – apart from waiters and so on. If they are working for the security apparatus, then they could be *agents provocateurs* who want you to say something critical about the regime, so they can pull you in and turn it into an incident. And if they're not Securitate, then they're putting themselves in grave danger. The whole place is riddled with informers. Some do it for money, others because the Securitate have some kind of hold over them. Either way, you and they are almost bound to be reported.'

'They wouldn't be bothered with me, would they?'

'Because you're just a secretary? I wouldn't rely too much on that. After all, they can take anything you say and twist it around, and use it against Mr Fleming, or the Legation.'

Clemency had met his type often enough; dislike or disapproval kept hidden behind a professional mask; and yet he would make sure she knew what he really thought. At least his manner suggested he had no idea of why Peter and she were there, and that was a relief. She trusted Peter, not this tedious man with his thinning hair and over-wet lips. Better if he made a pass at her than turning his flaccid lusts into disdain.

Nevertheless, his words added to her unease, as they were surely intended to do. Behind the excitement of a new city was this feeling of hidden surveillance. Everyone she saw around her could be the one to see through her disguise, guess why she was there, and so plunge her and Peter into disaster. In Bern, the Soviet danger had been abstract; here, with the blood-red banners of the Communist Party draped on every building, police on every corner, and everyone watching every word they spoke, she now understood something of the risks they were taking.

'I understand you'll be at a loose end tomorrow evening, while Mr Fleming is at the trade ministry reception. We do occasionally have English-language films presented in Bucharest. Nothing remotely political, of course, but comedies do very well. I believe the latest *Carry On* film is showing. I suppose it's the international language of smut,' he went on, pleased with himself.

'A quiet evening at the hotel will suit me,' she said crushingly. 'I'm sure there'll be a lot of correspondence to catch up on. It's a very full programme.'

'Actually, our Miss Fryer had suggested taking you under her wing tomorrow. She's a clerk in our chancery. That's the Legation's central registry for files. I expect she's keen to hear the latest London gossip.'

Clemency thought it highly unlikely that she would have come across this Miss Fryer in her previous life, the one before she became Caroline Green, and agreed that would be a very welcome distraction.

When Peter returned, she decided to have an early night and leave the men to more drinks. Heavy key in one hand, she found the lift, the fifth floor, the long gloomy corridor that led to her room. She realised that, for the first time, she was on her own, and it was a little unnerving; but also a release, a feeling that she could cope just as well, perhaps even easier, without worrying if she were doing or saying the right thing, staying in part, hitting the right note with Peter.

The rituals of undressing, cleaning her teeth, reading a few pages of her book, were comforting too. But after she switched out the light, she had to go to the windows, open the shutters, draw in draughts of the cool night air, and look over the city, the dark mass of Cişmigui Park, the tram rattling down the deserted street below, the two policemen strolling along on the other side of the road, hands behind their backs.

It was unfamiliar; perhaps dangerous; and what she felt most was the deep, welling sense of excitement that she had first felt in Feldsteen's study.

10

By the following evening, Clemency wondered if she had ever been so tired before in her life. The programme had been intense, but it was also the stream of unfamiliar things, places, people and experiences, starting with the breakfast of omelette and spicy sausage and pickled vegetables and the most intense, delicious sweet coffee that she had ever had, and which Peter explained was essentially in the Turkish style, Romania having spent centuries under Ottoman rule.

Coffee was the theme of the morning, as they moved from meeting to meeting. Each was the same. They would be welcomed outside a bland modern office block and taken to a spacious meeting room filled with heavy furniture and decorated with melancholy Romanian landscapes or uplifting portraits of worker-heroes of the Revolution. After the formal introductions, with much bowing and some gallantry towards Clemency – always the only woman present – there were exchanges about the weather, and how Bucharest was truly the Paris of the East, and the brave performance of the Czechs in the World Cup final, though Brazil were worthy winners, and then – daringly – the expression of the view that perhaps more exchanges in trade could bring the two nations of England and Romania a little closer and so promote international peace. And the coffee would arrive and Clemency would then concentrate on the job of noting down the exchanges and passing Peter the papers that he needed. The proceedings were in French, but Peter could follow most of it and she only needed to translate some of the more obscure words or idiomatic phrases. And after the statutory hour, they would be shown back to their taxi and off to the next meeting.

Clemency was shattered and also alive with caffeine, and when Peter had changed and gone off to the reception, she waited impatiently in the lobby, twisting the strap of her handbag, until a very fair, very English woman entered and looked about.

'Caroline? I'm Olivia. It's such a pleasure. We're like a leper colony here, so a new face is always welcome. I love your suit. Where did you get it? Everything here is hopeless. Though if I wore that to the Legation, the Ambassador would have a fit. Everything has to be below the knee, as if it were 1950. You must think I look such a frump.'

'Not at all.'

'That's so kind of you to say. Now, there's a place not far from here where we won't be pestered too much. Romanian men simply can't keep their hands to themselves. Worse than Berlin,' she added unexpectedly. 'This is quite simply a dreadful posting, but at least the food is good if you have foreign currency. Do you speak the language? It doesn't matter. Apart from ordering food and giving directions to the taxi driver, I never speak Romanian. If any of the ordinary people spoke to one, they'd be carted off and shot.'

Once they were settled in to a table at the café, and were handed their menus, Clemency could study her new friend without having to respond to her stream of thoughts. Olivia was a few years older than her, with lovely skin and blue eyes, and her hair in the style of two years before, and with the manner that spoke of acres round the house, horses and dogs. She reminded Clemency of Elizabeth, the Ambassador's secretary back in Bern, whose social *savoir faire* and organisation abilities had secured her the job, the career pinnacle for a Foreign Office clerk, at the comparatively early age of 35. Unless Olivia married, and so left the Service, that would be her future too, and she would do it well.

'I do like the look of your Mr Fleming. Ex-officer? Anyway, a proper gentleman. You can never tell with the commercial types. Not that we get many out here. Apart from whisky for the big-shot communist bosses, I don't think there's much they want from Britain, and I'm damned sure there's nothing they make here that we would want back home.'

'No?'

'No doubt they'd love to buy your trucks, but to be honest, I can't see where they'd get the money from. Which means they'll offer you goods in exchange. Tinned peaches, that sort of thing. Whatever you do, don't take their wine. It's not so bad here but I really can't see it traveling well.'

'Are your postings always this awful? Only I have a friend who is at the embassy in Bern and it sounds like a wonderful job.'

'Bern? Lucky thing. I hope she didn't have to do anything naughty to get it. Though I suppose it must be dull as hell. At least here you can think there's a point to it, we being on the front line, so to speak. It certainly feels as if we are under siege. Everywhere one goes, even coming out here with you, we're being watched. All the taxi drivers outside the hotels work for the Securitate. One of the waiters here will be an informer. There are microphones everywhere, even in the Embassy, even in my flat. It means you can never relax. Say your friend in Bern had a romance. Something discreet. There wouldn't be any worries if she took care of things. But here? Knowing some bloody little man was listening in to every sound? No thanks.'

'Can you travel around?'

'No, not even that. We're limited to ten miles of the capital. Apparently, it's the most beautiful country, but I'll never see it. Sorry to sound bitter, but it's so frustrating. A friend of my brother is the second officer on a liner and he says it's the same for him. You go to these wonderful locations – Cape Town, Colombo, Sydney – and you are stuck on the ship, you never see anything, or meet any of the locals. It drives him mad.'

'How much longer do you have here?'

'Eighteen months. The good thing is it's a hardship post so I should get a plum after this. I've heard a rumour it might be Rome. That's what's keeping me sane.'

'And what about Constanta? That's where we're going tomorrow afternoon.'

'We are allowed there sometimes. It has beautiful beaches, though I doubt you'll have much time for that, and the season's over, though the climate is mild. You're booked into the Hotel Palace, where a lot of the Party bigwigs go, so you should be looked after all right. It's where we stay. But whatever you do, don't let your guard down.'

'How do you mean?'

They were on their second glass of wine by now, and Olivia leaned forward confidentially.

'They have a kind of lido just down from the hotel. When I was there, I got chatting to one of the lifeguards. Little more than a boy, but the most wonderful body. Not too muscly, just right. And charm. Not turning it on like most of the men here. But he was learning English, and he was full of pride, and wanted to try it out on me. Nothing could have been more natural. He didn't make a big thing of it, but for the rest of the afternoon I couldn't stop looking over at him. And I started to think – why not? No-on would know. I'd say, I have a book I could lend you, come up to my room.'

'And did you?'

'I didn't sleep much that night, and the next day I went back for more. By then, he was in the pool with me, helping me to improve my technique, and then there was a bit of splashing, horse-play, you know the kind of thing.'

She sipped her wine, pushed her meal aside, and smiled reminiscently.

'I almost did, you know. And maybe it would have been worth it. But it would have been a full-on spy scandal. It's what they want. I'd have been sent home in disgrace, and that would have been the end of my time in the Service. And Trajan – that was the name he gave me, anyway – would have embellished our little fling with all sorts of attempts to subvert the constitution and recruit agents for sabotage and the rest of it.'

'But why you?'

'That's my point. They'll try it on everyone. Even you, if you're lucky,' she added with a smile. 'Certainly your boss. You know what men are like once they're past Dover. They don't think the same rules apply. Some little lovely, painted up to the nines, comes over and gets him to buy her a drink, and before you know it she's got him hooked. I bet you there are a couple of them in the bar of your hotel right now.'

'Now you mention it…' Clemency began, wondering at her own naivety, and whether she should warn Peter.

'Trajan,' Olivia said with a sigh. 'Like the emperor. And me feeling like his slave girl. Ridiculous. Anyway, just in time I had a call to come back to the hotel, there was a flap on back at the Legation, and I was packed and on a train back to Bucharest. A bit of luck, I suppose. That, or one of the other diplomats saw what was happening and tipped the Legation off.'

There had been a time when Clemency had thought she might let romance slip into something more serious, more physical, and that too had been a holiday romance. There was something so pleasurable in thinking about it, imagining standing on the edge of that particular plunge, toying with it, lifting one foot as if about to take that step.

It was how she felt now about Peter. She'd known that, of course, but the thought of him being seduced by the Securitate was just too painful.

'What about you?' Olivia broke in on her thoughts. 'You and your boss. Are you…?' She smiled, tipped her head on one side, taking the edge off such a personal question.

'No!' Clemency protested. 'Do people here think we are?'

'Not every businessman brings his own secretary. And those that do, well, it's not unknown. I expect if I saw the two of you together I'd know.'

'Don't. You'll make me self-conscious, and then you'll suspect the worst. Anyway, there's really nothing between us.'

'Yet?'

She had no intention of being as candid as Olivia. She wasn't under the same pressure of loneliness, the same tension, the relentless surveillance, the same need to fall upon the shoulder of a kindred spirit, even if one she hardly knew.

That night, the story of Trajan the life-guard merged with a couple of encounters from Clemency's own past, and with thoughts of Peter in a swimming pool, playing about, beads of water on his tanned skin, a knowing look in his eyes. But by morning, she was more excited by what the day would bring, because this would be the day that they made contact; and she could sit opposite Peter at breakfast without blushing.

As before, she talked him through the plans for the day, and the secret they shared, the unspoken reason why there were there, connected them much as if they were having an affair. Every comment, every glance, was steeped in double meaning, and it was impossible to think they could return to their old distanced selves when back in Bern, as had happened after the trip to Martigny.

At each meeting, Clemency was convinced that this would be the one where the Romanian comspirators would make contact. She waited for some sign of recognition, a moment at which Peter would be alone with one of the Romanian businessmen, away from the minders from the Ministry of Trade. But the only break from the formality was when Dimitri Petrescu, the assistant director of RomPort, spoke a little about the plans for their tour of the port of Constanta the next morning.

'You have come so far,' he said. 'We must show you a little traditional Romanian hospitality.'

He was small, tanned, with expressive eyes that were accentuated by his dark eyebrows and by his hair being nearly shaved across the rest of his head. He might have looked like a thug, but with him it humanised him a little, gave his expression an extra sensitivity. She could have imagined him as an actor, and for a moment she wondered if he was who he said he was, or was simply using the office, with its models of freighters under glass cases and its dramatic aerial views of wharves and cranes on the walls.

'I hope one day we will have the chance to do the same in England,' Peter was saying affably.

'Maybe I will one day come to England and to Stratford, to see where the plays of Shakespeare were first performed.'

'I would be delighted if that could be arranged,' Peter replied, not bothering to correct Petrescu; and Clemency was reminded of Eric Smithson talking about Shakespeare and the British Council, and its employees still rotting in jail all these years later. How kind and sensitive and humane you could be and still become a senior official in the Romanian state?

On the train journey she felt tired, out of sorts, unwilling to chat, even if Peter had wanted to do so. It was in part anti-climax: though he had said nothing, she was sure that the contact still had not come, and perhaps the whole thing was going to turn out to be a waste of time, like Paris. And as the countryside rolled by, flat and rich, with isolated stations, occasional glimpses of primitive villages still mainly built of wooden shacks, she felt she was a long way from London. And of course, she was. They were travelling further away from the airport, the British Legation, the tenuous links back to the West.

If it were a trap, surely Constanta – on the Black Sea, almost within sight of the Soviet Union itself – was the place it would be sprung.

11

The hotel stood on a grassy bank just a few metres from the sea, and they had rooms at the front, and Clemency opened the French windows onto the balcony and looked out over the calm expanse of the Black Sea, a wide horizon under the deep blue sky. With the sun setting behind her, the hotel made long shadows in front of her, right up to the empty beach.

Until the week before, when she had first learned that she would be coming to Constanta, she had never given the Black Sea a second thought. She had known of it, could probably have found it on a map, but never considered what it meant. Yet here in Romania, in Constanta, on this hotel balcony, was the end of Europe. To the south lay Turkey, fabled cities like Trebizond and Istanbul, the Middle East and Arabia. To the north and to the east, what was once the Russian Empire, now the Union of Soviet Socialist Republics – Georgia, Armenia, Uzbekistan – and the Golden Road to Samarkand.

She heard the connecting door open and then Peter was at her side.

'I know it's not Margate,' he said, 'but it doesn't feel like a totalitarian state when you're watching waves lapping on sandy beaches.'

It was as close as he had come to talking about the strains and tensions of their mission.

'You see all this building work?' He gestured towards the string of building sites, cranes and piles of steel stretching along the beach. 'You could be in

Monaco or Nice. I suppose it's the same, capitalist or socialist. You want to offer rewards – a week on a sun-lounger and cocktails by the pool. With us, it's your pay packet. Here, it's being a good party member. But those at the top have to have rewards to hand out, don't they?'

'I didn't think that you were so cynical.'

'No, and I don't get East and West mixed up on my moral compass. But I can see human nature at work on both sides of the Iron Curtain. I don't think the Communists are a different species.'

He seemed to want to say more; but there was every chance the room was bugged.

'Let's go for a walk,' she said. 'It's such a beautiful evening. And tomorrow will be a lot of work.'

They strolled for a mile or more along the path at the top of the beach, watching the sun sink, the shadows lengthen, and the other people around, mainly young couples, the women in bright cotton dresses, the men in white shirts with the sleeves carefully rolled up, on holiday but not entirely without status, judging by the chunky watches and the discrete jewellery.

They stopped for a while to watch a group of young men playing volleyball on the beach, all bare save for their swimming briefs and sunglasses. They were muscular, tanned, enjoying themselves; an unconscious advert for the teaching of Marx and Lenin. Then she noticed Peter giving her a sidelong glance, as if amused by her interest in the players.

'It's all a long way from fork lift trucks,' she said, turning away.

'The driver in Bucharest recommended a bar a little further along.' They walked on, passing the lido where Olivia had come close to being seduced.

'You're thinking of John Standfast, aren't you?'

It took her a moment to remember the code.

'No, not at all. Why? Is there something I should know?'

He leaned close, speaking low, though there was no-one about.

'What I love about you, Clemency, is that you are so good at actually not thinking about the job in hand. That's what we train our people to do when they're under cover, but most of the time they're still too self-conscious. They think, what should I be doing? What should I say? But you are so natural.'

She could strip away the condescension and was delighted with the praise inside. Could she persuade him that she should do this kind of work full-time? It was horrible to think that all this could be taken away from her again, as soon as they stepped off the plane at Heath Row, and that she would be sent back to decoding messages to other agents about other operations.

'Anyway,' he was saying. 'There's nothing new. I think the contact will be tomorrow. We're seeing this man Petrescu again and my guess is that the first meeting in Bucharest was a chance for him to check me out. With a bit of luck, he's reassured and will find a chance for a quiet word with me. Perhaps a tour of the docks, something like that. Or a drive to some outlying warehouse, if he trusts the driver not to listen in. If that happens, I'll send you back to the hotel.'

She didn't like the idea of being separated, but he was insistent. This was the moment of greatest risk, and he wanted her safely out of the way.

'You will take care of yourself, won't you?' she asked.

He stopped, held her by the shoulders.

'Clemency, please don't worry about me. This is a calculated risk. And the people doing the calculations, back in London, are the best in the business. If anything does happen to me, you know absolutely nothing. You're a secretary, nothing more and nothing less. Even if they were to pick you up, you just wait it out for a nasty few hours until the Embassy people get you out. Don't think you can help me by telling them anything.'

The reality of what he planned to do began to sink in. He could get into a car tomorrow and disappear altogether. However much the British protested, the Romanians could simply deny everything.

'No romantic nonsense about sacrificing yourself. OK?'

She managed a smile.

'Don't worry. I'm not Ingrid Bergman.'

'No, and I'm not Humphrey Bogart. You've got a job to do, and you're doing it damn well. I've got a job too, and without sounding conceited, I do have some skills and some experience. We plan in case something goes wrong. But it won't. Now, let's go and have that drink.'

◊

The programme for the next morning was less detailed than in Bucharest. The driver would collect them from their hotel at nine, and then it would be *meetings with senior officials* until *lunch with senior officials* and then an afternoon of *meetings with senior officials*. Peter was expecting this to include a visit to the port, but not that the car should take them on to one of the quays, where a group of men in dark suits and sunglasses were waiting for them. Peter wasn't exactly worried; but was pensive as one of the men opened the door for him.

Then he saw Petrescu approaching, his hand outstretched.

'Mr Fleming. And Miss Green. This is a great pleasure. Welcome to the Port of Constanta. And are we not so fortunate with the weather?'

He gestured to the calm blue sea, the cloudless sky.

'Splendid,' Peter replied. Clemency just smiled, but her eyes were drawn to the launch tied up close by. Although dwarfed by the merchant shipping of the port, it was still quite large, perhaps capable of crossing the Black Sea. To the Soviet Union, for example.

Petrescu followed her gaze, if not her thoughts.

'I have borrowed this from the Council of Workers' Recreation of Constanta. There is the port to be seen, and then we can continue our discussion as we sail up to the edge of the delta of the Danube. The wildlife is most exceptional.'

'I'd be delighted,' Peter replied, 'but I'm afraid that Miss Green won't be able to join us. There's so much to catch up on.'

'But I insist. Truly. You must not deprive us of her most pleasant company.'

'I'd love to oblige, but…'

'Unfortunately, the driver has returned to the hotel,' Petrescu pointed out. They were now alone on the quayside, except for Petrescu's two companions and the crew of the launch. Clemency saw sooner than Peter that if it were a trap, then protesting would achieve nothing. It was already sprung, and they were inside.

'I don't want to be any trouble, Mr Fleming. I'm sure I can catch up the work this evening. And it would be such a treat to see the Danube.'

'Then that is settled.'

'I suppose you've earned it,' he said, as smoothly as he could manage. 'You have worked very hard on this trip.'

'Miss Green,' Petrescu said, taking Clemency's arm. 'Whatever may happen in England, here in the Socialist Republic of Romania I will not have you exploited in this way. Come. I believe there will be some coffee.'

He guided her down the gangplank and through the saloon to the open area at the back of the boat. There were lockers covered with cushions around three sides, and an awning to provide some shade. That was welcome; even this early, the sun was fierce. Despite the possibility that they were being kidnapped with considerable courtesy, it would still be lovely to be out on the water.

The launch made a tour of the harbour, and Petrescu pointed out the main features, accompanied with endless statistics from the carrying capacity of the cranes to the cubic metres of silt removed in the most recent dredging operation that would allow the largest freighters in the Romanian and Soviet fleets to dock at any state of the tide. It was as if Petrescu was proving to Peter that he, too, had done his homework; for surely this was the contact they had come to make.

Then they set out further along the coast, and the white hotels and factory chimneys of Constanta sank out of sight, and there were low dunes, scattered trees, endless watercourses, flights of birds that Clemency could not recognise. There was no-one to be seen; no other boats; not even a freighter or liner on the far horizon. Suddenly, the sea seemed a lonely place.

'Has this been a successful visit for you, Mr Fleming?'

'I hope so, certainly. But I'm not impatient. You have to build trust before you can trade, don't you, and that takes time.'

Petrescu had arranged it so that he was sitting at the very back of the boat, with Clemency to his right, and one arm along the back of her seat. Wondering what was in a man's mind was second nature. She had decided that his personality demanded that a woman should be within his orbit, even if he had no particular interest in her. Certainly, all his attention was focused on Peter as they sparred about trade and trust.

The boat ploughed on, hardly troubled by the slight swell. Now it was clear they weren't going to be put into chains or thrown overboard, she could relax and enjoy the voyage, the scenery, the cooling breeze coming off the water. The conversation of Peter and Petrescu formed a pleasant enough background, like a wood pigeon calling on a summer's day.

'...*my country's position in the world is evolving...*'

'...*recent events in Berlin prove that Moscow and Washington must work together...*'

'...*under de Gaulle, France is showing you can hold your allies at a distance without betrayal...*'

Peter was enjoying himself, trading these coded statements with Petrescu. Both of them were leaning back on their cushions, expansive, with Petrescu the more animated, now using his hands to emphasise every point. And both, without being too obvious, were aware of Clemency. Not looking at her directly, certainly not expecting her to contribute thoughts of her own, but at some level conscious of the effect they were making on her. *I'm a mirror,* she thought to herself. *They're only glancing at me to see how they look*.

But Peter did look good; an unexpected situation, a conversation laden with double meaning, and yet he was relaxed. That one moment on the quay, when he had looked so disconcerted at the idea that he couldn't package Clemency off back to the hotel; was she, then, a liability to him, as he had said? Maybe he needed to trust her more, because she was the one who had smoothed over that difficulty, not him.

There was more conversation, more sea sliding by to one side and marshes to the other, and then Petrescu turned to Clemency and began to ask her about what concerts she went to, her favourite playwrights, novelists. She was on the point of telling him about a performance of *Don Carlos* she had seen, until she realised that had been in Bern. It was safer to fall back on jazz; though even here, Petrescu had his own views.

'In some circles, there was the idea that this jazz music was contrary to the principles of Marxism-Leninism. Now, we see it is the young choosing something new for themselves, as the young always do. But the way of dancing I cannot approve of.'

'Why is that?'

'You have a room, and everyone dances with everyone else. If I go out with a girl to a club, I want to dance with her and no other girl; and I want her to dance with me and no other man.'

There was more of this, a kind of examination, or an interview panel, with Petrescu putting the questions to her, and Peter now observing her reactions; Petrescu wanting to know if she could be trusted even with her marginal role in this affair; or if she were a weak link.

They passed a yellow buoy, rusty and slimy with

seaweed, stained with bird droppings, and then began a slow turn towards the land. Soon they were making their way up a creek lined with willows, until they came to a landing stage with a cluster of small boats tied up beside it. Petrescu gallantly handed Clemency down the gangplank and led the party to a café, where a table was laid out under a wide awning. There were two figures standing by the table, not talking, obviously waiting for them, the man short and round-faced, curly grey hair and an amiable expression that matched his rumpled suit; the woman very severe in a starched white dress with a high mandarin collar, her black hair cut in a bob. There were no other customers, in fact no-one at all in sight until another man, clearly the manager, hurried out to assure Petrescu that everything as ready for them, everything exactly as ordered.

Petrescu introduced the other guests: the man was Academician Cotescu and the woman Doctor Râs. The doctor had good English but nothing, it seemed, to say; instead she smoked and listened to the others intensely. Cotescu spoke a great deal of French in a most friendly manner. The atmosphere became a little less awkward.

After the glare of the sun on the water, the shade was very welcome. Clemency declined the offer of wine in favour of mineral water; the inevitable green bottle of Borsec. Then a car drew up and two men got out; one a senior officer, though Clemency couldn't identify the uniform; heavily-built, his hair cropped short, a stiff back. The other wore a linen suit and looked like a politician, although it turned out he was a senior Party official. Or maybe it came to the same thing.

During the meal, Clemency sorted out the relationships. All five of the Romanians – the conspirators, she might say – knew each other. Doctor

Râs and Victor Cotescu – whom the others called the Professor – were of lesser status; the General and Ion Mishcon, the Party man, were more powerful figures. Petrescu, though, was their equal, and also the moving spirit behind the endeavour. But it was hard to think of five more disparate characters.

Cotescu was a professor of Romanian literature; Doctor Râs the medical adviser to the Ministry of Foreign Affairs. The General held some unspecified post in the Romanian Air Force and the Party man, Mishcon, was the deputy general secretary of the regional Communist party. If there was an obvious connection, Clemency couldn't see it.

Mishcon sat next to Clemency, and though he couldn't speak English, they chatted for a while in French; though for all his outer confidence and his wide smile, he was the only one of them who was ill-at-ease. Perhaps he had more imagination and could picture what would happen to them all of the conspiracy were exposed. And then she thought of her own position, and realised Peter's concern for her safety hadn't been misplaced chivalry. If the Securitate were to burst in on them now, she might face prison, torture, a lifetime in jail. When she'd been on the quay, pressing forward had been fine; but this passive role of sitting over the meal, sipping the excellent wine, making polite conversation, tore at her nerves.

It was a relief whenever the conversation became general and – with the Romanians still speaking in French – she translated quietly for Peter when there was a word or phrase he did not know. But despite the language barriers, there was a lot of scrutiny. Perhaps even the way Peter drank his wine or ate his starter – a kind of gala pie that rejoiced in the name of *grob* –

was helping the Romanians decide how far to take this dance, how many veils to remove.

Once the plates were cleared and the wine glasses refilled, the General leaned forward, and at once the others turned to him for his lead. So far, he had said very little; been intent on fuelling his bulky frame with the excellent spread of fish and salad and cold potatoes. Now he began to close in on Peter.

'It is a great pleasure to have you here and I would not wish to spoil any of that feeling by talking of something such as politics. But there is one thing I would wish to know, my dear Mr Fleming, which is the feeling towards the Americans in your country.'

'To be honest, I don't think we think about them very much.'

'But they have their air force. They have submarine bases. They have many thousands of troops. Does this not feel a little like an occupation?'

'Not at all. You rarely see an American. They keep to themselves.'

'And the signs for the big American companies. For Coca-Cola and Ford and Esso. You have these on your buildings, on boards on the sides or the roads. Does this not feel like the symbols of a dominant empire?'

'Not at all.'

He nodded heavily, as if this were the answer he had expected; had wanted.

'Now Miss Green, when you first came to our country, to Bucharest, what did you make of the murals showing Lenin, the red star on the Palace of Culture, the hammer and sickle on our flag? Did they look like symbols of imperial dominance by a neighbouring country?'

'They made me think of Russia, certainly,' she

replied cautiously.

'And now? Do you feel we are slaves and the Russians our masters?'

'No.'

Satisfied, he returned to his meal; but she wondered how much of the plain-speaking grizzled army officer was an act.

Then the Professor leant over.

'As you speak such excellent French I wondered if you have ever read any of the poets of our country? I do not even know if they have been translated into English, but certainly there are French versions that do not lose all of the spirit of the originals.'

'I haven't, but I did begin a novel by Nitelea.'

'In Romanian? You speak the language?' The Professor was clearly delighted; no actor could fake his pleasure so completely.

'That's why I am so slow. I'm reading with the book in one hand and the dictionary in the other.'

'There is no better way to learn.' And he began something of a lecture on poets, authors, even playwrights and actors, interspersed with quotations.

When Clemency began to fade, he turned to gossip, lowering his voice.

'What do you make of the good doctor?'

'I've hardly spoken to her.'

'Her surname has two meanings in Romanian. Let us see which you think most appropriate. The first is you would say in English laughter, or happiness.'

The woman was watching Peter intently, her head a little on one side, as if studying a patient. Her face might have been carved from wax, there was so little expression.

'What is the other meaning?'

'I don't know the English word, but a kind of wildcat that lives in the Carpathian mountains. I believe these cats are big enough to kill a lamb.'

'A lynx,' Clemency said automatically, watching the doctor more closely now. Assuming she wasn't there to seduce Peter, was she the channel to the Romanian Embassy in Paris? Petrescu was the key, so it must involve the docks. Importing something from the Soviet Union, with the chance to divert it to the West? Perhaps aircraft, given the General's involvement. Was Mishcon, then, the connection with the Securitate? But then where did the Professor fit in?

The meal was drawing to a close. Petrescu stood up, tapping a glass gently for silence.

'In a few moments, we will need to return to Constanta. But I think we owe Mr Fleming the answer to a question I know he must have in his mind. He has come two thousand kilometres, far from home, alone except for the charming Miss Green. He has seen many factories, participated in many meetings. Now he will wish to know, will his journey be crowned with success. Yes?'

The question was to the five Romanians around the table. Clemency could not read their expressions, but there was no obvious dissent.

'So, we are agreed. We will trade. What, that is too early to say. I expect there will be an initial transaction, and when that has been delivered and paid for, then we will begin to proceed more quickly. Will this prove satisfactory to your principals, Mr Fleming?'

'They will be delighted.'

'Then, a toast.' Petrescu stood, waited while the others did the same. *'Salut noul nostru parteneriat.'*

'Salut noul nostru parteneriat,' they chorused, and

finished their drinks, and Clemency wondered exactly what they each thought they had agreed.

◊

On the way back, at a signal from Petrescu, the launch came to a halt about half a mile from the coast, out of sight of any other vessels, and lay rolling in the swell, the engine puttering quietly.

'It seems a shame to be so long on the sea and not to swim,' Petrescu said. 'And I will anticipate your objections by saying that I have made all arrangements, down to providing you with costumes.'

And so this surreal day took a further twist. A few minutes later, Clemency emerged from the saloon in a one-piece flowery swimsuit to find Peter and Petrescu waiting, both in the briefest of trunks. Petrescu looked very masculine, very toned, his tanned skin covered with fine black hair; but Peter was not put to shame; his frame was less compact, but his muscles were clear, no sign of a paunch. There was the white line of a scar across the back of one thigh; a wound; she wondered when she'd find the chance to quiz him about that.

She followed them in, rejoicing in the sudden cold of the sea, the banishing of the tension of the day. To think, that morning, she'd been worried that Petrescu was planning to drown them.

Petrescu was swimming away from the boat in a determined front crawl, Peter not far behind, and after a moment she stopped trying to follow them and instead turned over in the water and lay on her back, gazing up at the blue.

She had to admire Petrescu's ingenuity. Anywhere else – the car, the boat, the restaurant – they might have been overheard. Here, so far out to sea, there was no chance of microphones, or hidden cameras. And sure enough, the two men, when about fifty metres from the boat, began to tread water and to talk.

To make her interest less obvious, she swam a slow circuit of the boat, and by then they were returning. She knew Peter would not be able to say anything, at least until they were back in Bucharest, when they were due to have a final meeting with the trade attaché at the British Legation.

She waited for them to climb aboard, then followed them up the wooden ladder at the back. One of the crew had bought a pile of towels and Peter came over to her, grinning broadly, and passed her one as she pulled off her bathing cap and shook her hair. His eyes travelled over her and he swallowed. And then she knew the deal was done. Nothing he said; it was the look in his eyes, the physical hunger for her that she had glimpsed that night in his apartment.

The victor looking around for the spoils.

12

The BEA Viscount deposited Peter at a cold and wet Heathrow and he was not looking forward to the dreary coach trip into Victoria; but as he entered the crowded arrivals hall he was met by Waters, one of the department's drivers. He led Peter outside, exchanging some thoughts about West Ham's FA Cup prospects, to where Swan was waiting, surrounded by files in the back of one of the unmarked Rovers. They drove westwards along the A4, towards Reading, while the wipers squawked as they cleared the fine rain from the windscreen and Swan filled him in on the latest from the Legation in Bucharest.

'They made the pick-up, and we've decoded the instructions. It's as you said. The Romanians will give us a sample of their product. We'll assess it. If it's what they say it is, then we're in business.'

'What's the product?' Peter asked, stifling a yawn.

'A reel of magnetic tape. The kind you have for tape recorders. About twenty centimetres diameter and about two centimetres thick. Weighs a pound or less.'

'And what's on it?'

'It's probably best if I let the experts explain. But our Romanian friends want you to lead on the hand-over. France again, but in the Alps. Given they still have strong links with the French from pre-war days, that makes sense. We aren't going to tell DST, though. I'll take the flak on that if anything happens.'

'Someone to cover my back?'

'They said no to that as well, though I'm still in two

minds. But they want you to have the girl with you. The one you took to Romania.'

'What for?'

'They didn't say,' Swan said casually. 'Maybe they think it's better cover.'

Peter let it go. Petrescu's thinking was obvious. Clemency was a kind of hostage for his good behaviour, because Peter wouldn't pull any tricks while she was about. Which was fine – he had no intention of trying anything on – so long as everything else went according to plan.

Soon they were turning off the A4 just before Maidenhead and approaching the gates of one of the smaller outposts of the Signals Research Establishment. Behind the chain-link fence were neatly trimmed lawns, green-painted Nissan huts, low square concrete buildings. The corporal at the gatehouse directed them to where the 'London gentlemen' were expected.

They were met by a Colonel Maxwell, very military and dapper and not at all Peter's image of a boffin in uniform. But Maxwell seemed to know his stuff. He was Royal Artillery, presumably one of the Army's new breed of guided-missile experts.

He led them into his office, where a tall, supercilious man with very blond hair was waiting for them. Simon Fallon was the Balkans desk officer in the Foreign Office's research department, their end of the connection to SIS. Peter had been briefed by him before the trip to Romania, and decided he disliked him quite a lot. It was probably mutual, he thought, as they shook hands with surface cordiality. Meanwhile Maxwell ordered teas for them all, and then settled back at his desk, pen held between his two fingers.

'I should start by saying that the Establishment here

is very grateful for your bringing us this. It's exactly the kind of information we'd like to get our hands on.'

Swan made some polite noises and Peter said nothing.

'I won't ask anything about your side of the operation – we're calling it ROSEWATER, by the way – but I'll fill in some of the background.'

He got up and flipped back a long piece of cloth that was covering a map on the wall.

'The Soviets have a missile testing station here, on the Crimea peninsula. A place called Olenivka. A bit like our Boscombe Down combined with Woomera. They develop their rockets, then fire them out over the Black Sea, and they have a string of tracking stations from here to here. It's not their only site by any means, but it's still highly significant.'

He turned back to his class.

'Now, what do you gentlemen know about telemetry?'

'Assume we know nothing,' Swan replied for them all. Maxwell looked pleased; a natural lecturer with a captive audience.

'Well, the principle is very simple. If you were testing a new design of car, or even aeroplane, you can put all the test equipment – accelerometers, stress gauges, and the rest – inside the machine, and go along with it for the ride. You can read the dials, make notes, even take data and put it onto magnetic tape for later analysis.

'A rocket is different, of course. You still want to collect all that information, but it's nigh on impossible to fit test equipment and retrieve the data afterwards. It would be destroyed when the rocket crashes back to earth. Instead, you collect the data and send them back to earth by radio. Then you can record it onto tape and analyse it later, at your leisure. Follow?'

'I think so,' Peter said casually.

'You only have to think for a moment to realise how valuable this data can be. Say the Soviets are testing a new missile. With access to the telemetry, we could tell how fast it goes, its range, potentially its payload, its guidance system. And that could mean we could develop counter-measures or train our pilots in how to shake the thing off. Now I know what you're going to say: wouldn't the Soviets simply encrypt the data? But missiles are not exactly roomy. You've replaced the warhead with all the measurement kit, and there's no space left for encryption devices.

'Instead, they – and we – rely on directional radio waves, so that the footprint of the signals is limited, and ideally only your own people will be able to intercept them. That's why the seas around our own missile testing station on Harris are filled with Soviet trawlers. They don't catch many fish, and they have a surprisingly large number of aerials.'

The men indulged in some wry smiles.

'We have a number of listening stations in Northern Turkey,' Maxwell continued. 'They cover the Black Sea. They are some of the most valuable bases that we and the Americans have in this field. Even so, there's a limit on what they can pick up.

'That makes the Romanian angle so interesting. You see, they are very well-placed to collect Russian telemetry. The peninsula north of Constanta is only a few hundred miles from the Crimea.'

'Why would they go to all that trouble?' Peter asked. 'Why wouldn't they simply ask the Russians?'

'This might be more your area, Simon.'

Fallon now took the stage.

'The nature of the relationship between Romania and the Soviet Union is unequal,' he pronounced. 'The Soviets don't share their very latest technology. They like to make sure that their satellites don't forget that Mother Russia is the big bear and they are the cubs. But the Romanian posture has shifted in recent years, notably in respect of Sino-Soviet relations, and over COMECON trade. Our hope is that their intelligence apparatus is creating a bit of distance too. Not as far as a breach, but maybe making themselves a little space.'

'You're certain the Securitate are involved?' Peter asked, with a faint hint of doubt in his voice, just enough to ruffle Fallon's feathers.

'Not certain, of course, but all the indications point that way.'

'I'm not sure I can see what's in it for them,' Peter continued.

'Oh, that's clear enough. We offer is a back channel so that when formal diplomatic relations between Romania and the United Kingdom are compromised, we and they have another connection to fall back on.'

It might be true; it might be wrong. But if it were, Fallon wasn't the one who was putting himself in the sights of the Securitate; that honour fell to Peter. But he was done with twisting his tail.

Colonel Maxwell drew them back to the main subject

'Assuming the first transaction goes well, I understand there may be a chance to influence the selection of material that might follow. For us, ground-to-air missiles are the priority. The RAF are switching their V-bombers to low-level and we just don't know enough about Soviet capabilities in this field.'

There was more, much more, of this before Colonel Maxwell was done. Peter struggled to keep awake. But he did at least have a question ready for when Maxwell was done, just to show he was on the ball.

'How will I know if the tape is the real thing?'

'You won't,' Maxwell replied with a faint smile. 'Magnetic tape all looks the same. Even if you played it on a standard tape recorder, all you would hear would be meaningless jumble of noises. Just get the thing back here and we'll do the analysis.'

The briefing done, Swan ignored Fallon's hints about getting a lift back to London and he and Peter returned to where Waters was waiting with their car. He was standing next to a large sign saying No Smoking, his hand cupped round his cigarette to provide some plausible deniability, a hangover from his Army days. He straightened, flicked it away with a practiced hand and opened the door for Swan. As Peter climbed in the other side, he saw Fallon at the far end of the block of offices, glancing at his watch, presumably waiting for a car to take him to the station.

'What do you make of it all?' Swan asked, once they were through the gates and on their way. 'These five Romanian bods sound like a pretty rum bunch.'

'It might be a blind,' Peter ventured. 'If it's, say, just Petrescu and the General, then having the others there makes it less obvious.'

'And you're sure Petrescu is Securitate?'

'He's certainly not just deputy director of the Port of Constanta. He's a player. Someone of substance. The General and Mishcon treated him as an equal.'

'What about this woman doctor? What on earth was she doing there?'

'I did wonder if there was some kind of germ

warfare angle, but it doesn't sound like that now. Maybe she is important for shipping the consignment out of Romania, especially if they're using the diplomatic bag.'

It was Clemency who had suggested this, but telling Swan that would only confuse things.

'And this academic? How does he fit in?'

'Hard to imagine. Maybe he was there to size us up?'

Swan gazed out at the factories that lined the road.

'There's something about all of this I don't like,' he said in the end. 'Or am I turning into an old woman?'

'I just can't see their motives,' Peter replied. 'The money? How are they going to spend it? Are they all going to defect *en masse?* And if one comes over, all his associates are going to be tarnished. It just looks like one hell of a risk for them.'

'Yes, and my guess is that the data they sell us will be faked up in some way. It will either overstate the missile's capabilities to spook us, or understate it so that it's more dangerous than we thought if it ever came to a shooting war. But the good news is that it will be for Maxwell and his boffins to make sure we're not duped, and he is well aware of the risk.'

Peter nodded, reassured. He wanted to go. This was the kind of case that didn't come along very often, and personal and professional pride was pushing him on. If it came off, it would be one of the two or three most significant coups of the year. He wasn't going to pass that on to someone else.

But bringing Clemency in was another matter. She trusted him, and he hated the thought of anything happening to her.

'Back to the girl. What do I tell her? She's cleared

up to Secret.'

'Tell her? Nothing, of course. She doesn't need to know, does she? Just hang on your arm.'

'Yes, but what if there's any rough stuff?'

Swan found this funny.

'Well, if there is, the last thing you should do is worry about her. If this stuff is as good as they say it is, then it's gold dust. And we've no shortage of cypher clerks.'

Peter thought – hoped – that Swan was joking.

13

In the early afternoon, Clemency was decoding an urgent ACTOR telegram when she came across one of Peter's cover names. She remembered it only because he'd joked about being called AJAX: was he a Greek hero or something to clean the floors? The rest of the message meant nothing, even in clear, but it was an excuse to go out to the airport to meet his flight once her shift was finished. And having the telegram, sealed in a stiff buff envelope, made the meeting less awkward. They were just two colleagues, nothing more.

He took the envelope, tore it open. His face gave nothing away, but she noticed how tired he was.

'Thanks,' he said briefly, folding it up and placing it in his jacket pocket. 'And it's a bit of luck, you being here. We can talk on the way back into town.'

They walked over to the airport car park. His MG stood on the far side, all on its own, and despite the good weather he'd put a tarpaulin over it. She said something teasing about having to get a proper car with an actual roof, but he gave her a rather superior smile in return.

'It's an old trick,' he said. 'I put this on, folded just so, and if anyone's been tampering with the car, I'll know. That way, no-one cuts the brakes, or puts a bomb under the front seat, and I get a year closer to my pension.'

He walked round the car, making it look casual, and then pulled off the grey cover and folded it up into the boot, placing his single small suitcase on top.

She wondered what it would be like, living with the ever-present risk of assassination, needing to take these kinds of precautions. She'd found the last few days wearing enough, always wondering if someone was watching her, or whether she was being trailed. Even with her lessons from Lucinda, she knew she was vulnerable. And when she had climbed into the passenger seat, she still had a moment of unease as Peter turned the ignition.

'So, the news is, we're going skiing.'

He gave her a briefing on the mission, and her own role, but although she was nervous and excited in equal measure, she was alkso puzzled.

'Is there something you're not telling me?' she asked. 'I don't mean I have to know everything,' she added hastily. 'Only, you don't seem happy.'

'Yes, but it's nothing to do with you.'

She didn't reply. He concentrated on the traffic, as they entered the outskirts of the city, cutting in between the lanes in a way that a Swiss driver would never do.

'It's one of my chaps,' he said at length. 'Stanêk. He's coming over. Tomorrow morning. It was supposed to be in a couple of weeks. That's what the message wqas about. Something's spooked him.'

'Over?'

'The border. From Czecho. I'll need to be there.'

She pictured the miles of fences, barbed wire, watchtowers, armed guards patrolling. The front line of the Cold War, stretching from the Baltic to the Black Sea.

'How far is it?'

'To Schirnding? Oh, about eleven hours. If I start by eight I'll be there in good time.'

'Driving through the night? Don't be silly. You're so tired already.'

'Are you volunteering to drive me?'

'I'd only be going to the *Alabama*. You might be saving me from a long-haired Beatnik.'

Peter didn't put up much resistance. She picked up her passport and an overnight bag from her flat, he did the same at his while she waited in the car, and they were on their way. He fussed about how she should watch the cluch and be gentle with the steering but she ignored him and concentrated on getting a feel for the car. Within half an hour, as the sun began to set, he stopped speculating on whether it would be better to go via Stuttgart or stay on his original route through Munich and Augsburg and began to snore gently.

He woke when she stopped for supper at a roadside café, and again at the West German border, but she took it as a compliment that he could sleep at all with a girl at the wheel of his beloved car. She didn't push the speed, because they didn't need to be at the station at Schirnding until ten o'clock. Peter had explained that this was not a mad dash across the wire, dodging bullets and land mines. Stanêk had all the right papers and would simply board the train in Prague, show his papers on the border at Clud, and then step down at Schirnding into Peter's waiting arms.

Once night had fallen, the drive was very peaceful. The roads were good, and largely empty, and the car ran well. Peter had fitted a radio, and she found an evening concert of Bruchner and Brahms. And there was Peter himself, looking so much younger in his sleep, so that she felt very protective of him.

At two in the morning, she began to feel sleepy and stopped at a rest area off the *autobahn* where there was a kiosk selling coffee. Only then did she realise that she had no Deutschmarks, but the man behind the counter waved her Swiss francs away with a laugh.

When she returned to the car, Peter was awake. He took the remains of her coffee and drained it, then insisted on taking the wheel. He did seem so much more himself, and she happily snuggled down into his coat and closed her eyes and let him finish the long haul north towards Regensburg.

◊

They sat in the station buffet, Peter tackling a plate of sausage, Clemency feeling that a stale pastry filled with marzipan was as much as she could cope with at that hour. They read the papers and tried not to look at the clock too often, until the train was called.

They went onto the platform and Clemency looked beyond its end to the expanse of lines and sidings, signals and gantries, beyond which lay Czechoslovakia. After a while, she could make out the white headlight approaching, frustratingly slowly, and at last the train was rolling past them. There was little glamour in the drab green and grey carriages pulled by a scruffy diesel engine, though it had come from Istanbul and it was going to Paris and was still listed in the timetable as the *Orient Express*. Some passengers stepped down for some fresh air, or to reassure themselves that they were away from the grip of Communist totalitarianism. But Staněk wasn't one of them.

They walked into the main square to the post office, and Peter made some calls, while Clemency sat on a bench outside in the December sunshine and tried not to fret.

At last, he came out and waved to her. He was already striding back towards the station and she had to run to catch up.

'There was a patrol on the train and he panicked. He got off in Cheb, just over the border. Now he's stuck there.'

'Can he go back to Prague?'

'Risky.'

Peter was talking to her, answering her questions, but he wasn't really listening. His mind was elsewhere. Planning.

'Peter, what are you going to do?'

He ignored her, ploughing on towards the ticket office.

'Peter, you know you can't help him, don't you?'

'Do I?' he snapped.

She hung back while he bought a ticket and rooted through his attache case, selecting a bundle of papers. He came over and handed it to her.

'I'm sorry, Clemency. I don't mean to be a beast, but there's not much time. Look after these papers. I'll be back on the 16.17. And if I'm not, call this number and ask for a man called Swan. Tell him what's happened. But don't call before then and don't even think of coming after me.'

◊

The waiting was the worst. Almost six hours. She was convinced she would never see him again. It was impossible to believe he could just walk across one of the most secure borders in the world, pick up a defector and stroll back again. He couldn't have been entirely unprepared, because he had left his own passport with her, and must have a set of false papers. But it was still an act of impulse, unplanned, risky beyond belief.

She sat in the buffet, with a coffee she couldn't drink, couldn't even bear to look at as it cooled and a skin formed on the surface. She was all of those women in all those war films, waiting at home for her pilot husband or boyfriend to come back, and knowing one day he wouldn't, that instead there'd be a telegram, informing her that he was missing in action. Or a knock on the door from one of his pals from the squadron, saying that it was a rotten shame but he'd got the chop over Bremen or Hamburg. And she'd be so brave, because that's what he would have wanted.

She couldn't play that role. Instead, she took his car and drove out of the town, taking a succession of side roads at random. She stopped in some woods and began to walk fast, trying to leave her fears behind, almost succeeding, until she realised she was lost and half-ran back to the track where she'd left the car.

She drove south, then east, until she came to the border. It formed a great scar across the fields and woods, because they had torn up every tree and hedge, torn down every house, barn and wall, for a hundred yards or more on either side to form a killing ground. The scale of it scared her, the sheer force it displayed, where even the guards patrolling it with guns and dogs were made insignificant. This was what Peter had challenged, because he felt a responsibility to this unknown agent.

For the first time, she realised the kind of man Peter was. London might think it was expedient to sacrifice an agent or two, like the staff at the British Council in Bucharest. But Peter was risking his life to bring Stanêk out.

Somehow, by being parked by the road, as close as she could to the border, she was giving him some kind of moral support. It comforted her, and she relaxed. Let her eyes close.

Then there was a man tapping on the window, waking her. A policeman, or a border guard, telling her to move off. She gathered that sightseers made them nervous, as if they were going to cause trouble. She quickly smiled and nodded and started the car and was in any case near to panic again about getting back to Schirnding, about whether she had enough petrol, whether he had left her enough money.

In the event, she was there with two hours to spare, furious with herself for getting in such a state. None of this was going to help Peter.

She pulled into the car park and began to wonder how she could possibly pass the time, when he opened the passenger door and climbed in.

'Where on earth have you been?' he said. She was so surprised he burst out laughing.

'My God, Clemency, your face! I'm sorry, but that was priceless. Anyway, come on, let's get going. It's a long run home.'

'What happened to Stanêk?'

But she hardly needed to ask. Peter was in such tearing high sprits he'd obviously succeeded. He explained that he'd found him almost at once, sitting disconsolately in a bar near the station, and they'd caught the next train. There had been nothing but a routine check at the border, and they'd been back in West Germany within two hours of his setting out.

'I've used the route before,' he said. 'I have a contact on the railways who lets me know if there's any unusual security activity. He thinks I'm a smuggler. In fact, the only hitch was waiting for you to come back. Stanêk stayed on the train. We'll meet him in Basle and you can take the train from there.'

He was far too keyed up to sit passively in the passenger seat, even if there weren't two hours to make up on the *autobahn*. They swapped seats and set off. After a few minutes, she could find some words.

'Peter, I'm very glad to have you back.'

Though he didn't take his eyes from the road, his slightly conceited grin returned.

'Good. But you didn't think I'd let the nab me, did you? Remember, you and I have a weekend in the Alps coming up.'

14

Peter was like a young boy with maps spread across his dining table and lists of all the things they would need.

'There's a hard top for the MG, and a chap I know ran me up a ski rack for it. Saves us hiring when we get there.'

'I don't have any skis.'

'Oh, I'll borrow some for you. Gail Pemberton and Annette Dansby-Greg both ski.'

Clemency wondered how Peter would explain why he wanted them. At least Mrs Dansby-Greg wouldn't be shocked at the idea that he was having an *affaire*. And surely Peter of all people could be relied on not to give away who he was going with. That was one advantage of having an *affaire* with a spy. Was that what it was, or was going to become? In a chalet, with a storm raging outside, flickering firelight and sheepskins rugs?

'You have skied before, though?'

'Oh yes.' She dragged her mind back to the present. 'Cross-country and downhill. Daddy used to take us to Cauterets, in the Pyrenees.'

'Lucky you. St Quentin is higher, and you get a lot more sun, so you'll need a proper thick jacket and some really good Polaroid sunglasses. What sort of boots do you have?'

Clemency was more concerned by what she would wear off the slopes. The magazines were always showing film stars and singers and fashion designers in St Quentin. What if she were at the next table to Deborah Kerr or Grace Kelly, wearing one of the dresses she had made herself using a pattern from a magazine? Or she bumped into Dirk Bogarde on the slopes in her disreputable old tartan jacket and woollen cap?

Meanwhile Peter was asking her about knapsacks and Thermos flasks.

'What about the actual hand-over?' she said. 'What if it goes wrong again?'

'We'll be fine. I'll give you the details nearer the time, but they've thought it through pretty well.'

She looked at the map. The village itself was high up in the mountains, surrounded on three sides. Thin lines marked the cable cars and ski lifts, but though you could ski over to the neighbouring villages of St Yves and Montlucan, there was only one road in our out, snaking its way up the valley along the line of the Chevalle. From the main road, it was then another ten kilometres back to the Swiss border.

'If I were them, I'd let us pick up the package and then jump us on the way out.'

'It's not the Wild West, you know,' he laughed. 'Anyway, I won't be entirely defenceless. And that reminds me – I was going to give you your first lesson, wasn't I? There's no time like the present.'

They had lunch in the café on the corner and then drove out to the range in the afternoon. It was a long, low brick building down a track off the main road, screened by trees and surrounded by a hefty chain-link fence. Inside, it was a little like a sports club, except that with golfers or rugby players there would have been more chatting, joking, raised voices. Here the men looked serious and competent, talking shop or quietly disassembling and cleaning their weapons, and she couldn't imagine them swilling down pints of bitter once they were done with their day's sport.

There was a very faint scent of gunpowder in the air, as if it were the day after a fireworks display. Peter was clearly at home there, and nodded to several of the other members as he booked them in. She felt self-conscious, aware of the glances she was attracting. She imagined the few women who came here as tall, blonde amazon types, in bush shirts, boots and jodhpurs, not a turtleneck sweater and cotton skirt.

They took their places at one end of the range. Peter fitted some sheets of thick paper printed with concentric circles into a contraption that reminded Clemency of the clothes lines strung over the narrow alleys in Paris. He pulled on one of the ropes, and the targets moved down to the far end of the range.

He began his lesson.

'The thing about handguns is that they're very noisy and very, very inaccurate. You really only want to use them to frighten people. That means looking confident. I don't want to turn you into a crack shot – that would take far too long anyway – but I want you to feel sure of yourself. That way, if you ever have to start waving the thing around, people will take you seriously and do what you say. Right?'

Brisk, business-like, he picked up the gun and began to show her how it worked: naming the parts, demonstrating the mechanism for loading and unloading, the operation of the safety catch and trigger mechanism. She liked being taught things, and he was a good instructor; clear, firm, but not unfriendly. When at last he took the gun from her and began to load it with bullets, she was surprised to see that half an hour had passed.

'Here's how you hold it.'

He took her hand and folded it around the butt of the

gun, his grip warm.

'The trigger has a spring. You need to apply a certain amount of pressure before it will fire, and that varies a lot from gun to gun. Professionals care about that stuff. For our purposes, you just want to squeeze it firmly. Like this.'

He stood behind her, lifted her hand and pointed it at the paper target, thirty feet away. With his arm against hers, his chest against her back, even his legs braced against hers, she felt very safe.

'Then you just pull the trigger.'

The gun fired. Her hand jerked up a little, and despite herself she gave a little yelp of surprise. Then she saw a small, ragged hole on the very edge of the target.

'Not bad. Let's do it again.'

They fired off the remaining six rounds, with only one missing the target altogether, and the rest coming a little closer to the centre.

'Very good. The secret is that you have to want to pull the trigger. I mean, don't think this is a big awful noisy scary thing. Think that this is a tool that you know how to use, and you want to use it. You're making it go bang. You're in charge. Got it?'

'I suppose so.'

'Right.' He took the gun, stepped away, reloaded it, then handed it to her. 'Five rounds in the target.'

Without his presence, her back felt chilly and the gun seemed heavy in her hand. But she raised it to the imaginary line from her eye to the bullseye and squeezed the trigger. Though the barrel lifted at each shot, the bullets at least hit the target, even if more spread than when Peter had been holding her.

'Not bad.' He spoke lightly, but he was impressed.

'Let's hope I never have to do this for real.'

'Don't worry about that,' he said. 'Remember what I said. Our world is fundamentally dull.'

◊

Without actually saying so, Peter had given her the impression that they shouldn't be seen together too much in the days leading up to the trip to St Quentin. So she was surprised when he phoned down on Friday morning and asked her to come up to his room; and even more surprised to find that Peter was not alone. Cedric Dansby-Gregg was there too, looking particularly acidulated.

'Ah, Miss White,' he said, as if he had uncovered the route of his problems. She wondered what she had done wrong, and how Peter fitted into it.

'Have a seat.' Peter's tone was more welcoming, but there was still a hint of the headmaster's study in the air.

Dansby-Gregg sat behind Peter's desk and opened up a slim buff folder. Peter perched on the edge of the desk, swinging a leg casually. Dansby-Gregg looked put out, but could hardly say anything.

'Now, Miss White. May I start by confirming that you have read the security instructions for staff on overseas postings.'

'I have,' she said cautiously. Was this about a security breach? Had she left a classified document on her desk overnight, or the keys in the lock of one of the many filing cabinets? It was easy enough to do; but rarely would it involve someone senior like Dansby-Gregg.

'Do you recall the section about reporting contacts with nationals of Communist states?'

'I do.'

It was so tempting to say that, only a few weeks

before, she had been lunching with senior officials of the Romanian government; but presumably Peter wanted that kept under wraps. Either way, Dansby-Gregg was about to make a monumental fool of himself.

'Are there any contacts that you might have forgotten to report? That you would like to tell us about now?'

She hesitated. He knew something damaging to her, or thought he did. But what could she say?

'No.'

He made a note on the file; she resisted the temptation to look to Peter for reassurance.

'We have received information from a reliable source about a meeting you had with a Soviet official on 23 October. Last Thursday. Around 8.45 in the morning.'

'This must be a mistake.' She could hear anxiety in her own voice. 'I've never spoken to any Russians since I got here.'

'Maybe this will jog your memory.'

He slid a photograph across the table to her; a large, 10 x 8 print, showing a row of houses, a couple of parked cars, the trunk of a tree and two figures strolling along together. The woman was young, fair, her hair cut short, wearing a macintosh open over a suit. It did look a bit like her, she supposed.

The man was looking away from the camera, towards the woman, but—

'Oh, him. But he was French. And he was just asking me the way.'

'Really? But you walked with him for upwards of seven minutes.'

'Was it that long?'

'What did he say his name was?'

At last, Peter leaned forward.

'Perhaps Miss White should explain what happened

in her own words.'

'Of course,' she said gratefully, and again Dansby-Gregg looked irritated. He was enjoying playing the District Attorney, trying to break the alibi of a notorious gangster, and Peter was ruining his fun.

'Well, it's all so silly. I came out of my flat and was on my way to work and he stopped me and asked me where the Zuidstrasse was. I told him how to get there, but he looked a bit blank, and because it's on my way to work I said I'd show him. We walked along for a bit, and then we got to the corner of Englegasse and I could show him the entrance to Zuidstrasse and he thanked me and took himself off.'

'What did you talk about?'

'I can't really remember. I think he explained he was visiting Bern and kept getting lost. And then he asked if it was a rather dull place for a young woman, and I said there was plenty to do, and I think I said something about the jazz club by the old market.'

'A jazz club.'

'That's right. And I think he said he preferred the opera. It was all like that. Utterly inconsequential.'

'Did he ask you where you worked? What your job was?'

'No.'

'Nothing?'

'Nothing.'

Dansby-Gregg was dissatisfied and stared down at his file in irritation.

'What was he like?' Peter asked.

'Ordinary. About forty. Clean-shaven, neatly dressed. He wore a raincoat over a suit. A hat. A Homburg, I think. I don't think he was carrying anything.'

'But what was he like? As a person?'

'To be honest, I thought he was a bit of a creep. I mean, why ask me? I wasn't the only one on the street. And he was just a bit too eager when I said I could show him the way.'

'Did he ask where you lived?'

'No, but I suppose he could have seen when I came out of the flat. But who is he?'

'Is this the man?' Dansby-Gregg slid another photograph over. It showed a man in half-profile, locking or unlocking a car. Like the other photograph, it was taken from a distance, without the subject knowing; and was grainy, a bit blurred. But it was definitely the same man.

'Who is he?'

'His name is Konstantin Petrov. He's a colonel in the GRU. Until last year he was the GRU's resident in Bern.'

'So why was he asking me the way?' It was a stupid question, and she began to blush; but Peter continued to help her out.

'My guess is that he wanted to size you up. Plus, he could pretend to run into you again, and do the usual pick-up stuff – what a coincidence, small world, have you time for a drink, all that jazz.'

'But why me?'

Again, it was a stupid question; particularly with Dansby-Gregg there. Obviously, Peter hadn't said anything about her work for him, and she needed to follow his lead.

'As Mr Aspinal says, it might have been to size you up. Perhaps they thought you might be the type to be open to, er, seduction. It has happened before, you know – a girl on her first posting, at a loose end, drawn into romance.

'He'd have been the last man on earth to seduce me,' she replied.

'Why do you say that?' Peter asked.

'There was something definitely wrong about him.'

'Can you be more specific?' he insisted, and as it was Peter asking, not Dansby-Gregg, she tried to put her impressions into words.

'He was the kind of man who… who would enjoy gaining an influence over you. He'd try all the tricks. Say at a party, he'd be making little snide comments about you that sounded like a joke but had a sting in them. He'd be niggling away at your confidence. He'd have to be in control – asking where you went, who were your friends. Making a scene if you spent time with them, because he'd want you to be isolated.'

'It sounds as if you got to know him rather well in the few minutes you were together,' Dansby-Gregg drawled.

'I don't think it takes very long to know what men are really like,' she replied, and Dansby-Gregg reddened.

'You haven't seen him since,' Peter said, his voice a little strained, so that she guessed he was having trouble trying not to laugh.

'No. But if I do, I will report it at once. Now that I know he's a Russian.'

'I should be most grateful if you would,' Dansby-Gregg said. 'And please do not mention this to anyone. The Swiss spotted that he was back in Bern and set up a surveillance. They shared the results informally with us on the strict understanding that it would be treated with the utmost discretion. We really couldn't have this the subject of gossip in the clerks' room.'

'Don't worry about that, Mr Dansby-Gregg,' Clemency said sweetly. 'We have plenty to gossip about without talking about Russian spies.'

Her barb struck home; he gathered up his papers and left, so that Peter and Clemency were left looking at each other.

'That was very naughty of you,' he said quietly.

'Seeing the Russian? How was I to know?'

'No, making fun of his wife.'

'Oh, he deserves it. He's so boring. No wonder she plays around.'

'Plays around. Is that how a well-brought up young lady should speak?'

Peter might want to flirt, but she was still thinking of the photos.

'I feel so stupid that he could talk to me like that and I had no idea who he was.'

'Well, he is a professional.'

'He seemed so harmless.'

'He's anything but that. In fact, there's a rather nasty story about Petrov. I had it from a chum in the VVD. It seems Petrov was put into Hungary after the '56 uprising. Lots of combing through the state apparatus for any reactionaries and counter-revolutionaries. And a chance for people to settle old scores. Anyway, it seems there was this girl cypher clerk in their Ministry of Foreign Affairs. She'd done a posting overseas – somewhere like Norway – and that was suspect in itself. This man Petrov decided she was guilty and was lining up a show trial or a disappearance, but her uncle was high-up in one of the ministries and stepped in to stop it. Instead, Petrov arranged to meet her on the Buda bridge, and when she got there he just grabbed her, picked her up and threw her over the edge. And then – this is the really nasty bit – he got the post mortem changed to show she was pregnant, and claimed she'd confessed that her uncle was the father of the child. So, he was arrested, tried and executed too.

'And Petrov made sure it was known. It was a message. Don't get in my way.'

'But Peter, why would this man be bothered with me? Do you think he knows something about Paris?'

'I don't think so. It will be as Dansby-Gregg says; they're looking for someone vulnerable at the Embassy to try and trap. Next thing will be a tall blond charmer who'll sweep you off your feet and into his bed, where you'll find yourself unburdening yourself to him over the pillow.'

'Seriously, Peter. If they know I'm working for you, then I can't be of any help in St Quentin, can I? They'll follow us.'

'Are you saying I should go with Joy instead? Or Annabelle?'

She hesitated for a moment.

'Yes. I think you should.'

He slid off the desk and stood over her, that look of exasperated affection back again. She used it herself, sometimes, with the family dogs. Was that how she seemed to Peter, staring up with pleading eyes, desperate to be taken for a walk, and desperate not to upset her master.

'Don't worry.' He touched the end of her nose. 'Go home and get packed.'

15

The winter sun was shining as they crossed through the Alps to the French border; which was just as well, because the car's heater couldn't compete with the chill breeze and when they were in the valleys, in shadow, the cold seeped into Clemency's bones. She thought her coat would be enough; she wished she had taken up Peter's offer of a blanket.

Still, the drive was beautiful, and the car could handle the gradients and the hairpin bends, and Peter was a very good driver, so there was the thrill of seeing a thousand feet drop just beyond the low parapet of the road, and yet the security of his hands light but firm on the wheel, his eyes set on the road, his mouth in a faint smile, because he was enjoying it too – and in a mild way, enjoying showing off to her.

The road was clear of snow, but it lay in broad patches over the rocks and the thin grass, and further away the mountains glittered a blinding white under the blue sky.

There was hardly any traffic on the road; but when they reached the border post, as if by magic a queue appeared. They slotted into the end and Peter turned off the engine.

She wondered where his gun would be stashed; assuming he had brought one. Did the car have a hidden compartment – one that even experienced customs officers would not find? Or would his diplomatic passport be enough?

'Have you ever crossed the border between Belgium and Holland?' he asked conversationally. 'You just drive straight through.'

'They don't stop you at all?'

'No, it's their Benelux Union.'

The cars in front inched forward. Peter stayed where he was, until the moral pressure from the cars behind became too much, and he switched on the engine and closed the five-metre gap.

'The Pembertons are very generous in lending out their chalet and I usually come out here for a week in January. There's no better way of putting Christmas and New Year behind you than eight hours on the slopes, day after day.'

She wondered who he had stayed here with; and that opened up whole secret corridors and locked doors of Peter's life.

'When I first started coming,' he went on, 'you used to see so many familiar faces. Of course, that was back when the British could afford it. It's all Germans and Italians now. And Americans. Anyway, the chalet is very discreet. It will be good to have a proper base, particularly after Paris. Hotels are far too open.'

Very discreet. Was his choice of words a coincidence, or was there something else in his mind beyond espionage? Facing up to the GRU she could take in her stride, but the thought of taking that particular plunge with Peter was alarming.

'You look frozen,' Peter said. 'There's coffee in the flask in the back.'

She turned around in her seat and reached over to grab a knapsack with the neck of a Thermos sticking out. There was a tingling moment of intimacy as she brushed against his hand with her thigh. She stretched just a little further to draw that moment out.

'Sorry.'

'Not at all.'

Then she was wriggling back into place and demurely pulling down the hem of her skirt before pouring them both a cup of coffee.

'This smells lovely,' she said.

'Yes. It's from the Italian delicatessen on Cramgasse. Whatever else one might say about the Italians, they do know their coffee.'

His hand hadn't… *explored*. But he hadn't withdrawn it, either. For months now, ever since the first kiss in his flat, she had both wanted more and been scared of where it would go. Still there was no answer as to what he himself intended. But that was all part of the anticipation.

'How far to St Quentin?'

'An hour on these roads. I wish you had a better coat than that.'

This was made of thick red tartan with a fur collar and had a hint of a Canadian lumberjack. She had always liked it; and even if she wanted to change, there was no way she could afford a new one. But he seemed unaware of her sudden embarrassment, the thought that she would be showing him up at the resort.

'You never told me what happened to Stanêk,' she said, to change the subject.

'Oh, he's fine. The things is…'

Suddenly Peter was looking embarrassed: very unusual for him.

'Well, I was going to tell you at the chalet. A bit of good news. Rather than send Stanêk on to London, I passed him to the Swiss to debrief. His thing is industrial espoinage, which the Swiss intelligence people are keen on, so they were rather grateful.'

'Can you really swop agents like that?'

'Up to a point,' he said evasively. 'Anyway, in return, they've done a favour for me. You as well. They've deported Feldsteen.'

It took a moment for it to sink in.

'That's right. No more looking over your shoulder. Last I heard he was back in Mexico. And the best of it is, he won't have any idea I was behind it.'

She flung her arms around him.

'Oh Peter, I can't believe it. I hadn't wanted to say how scared I was but…'

He held her for a while, then gently detached her.

'Won't London be furious with you?' she asked, dabbing away her tears of relief with a handkerchief.

'Only if I tell them. Now, have you left me any of that coffee?'

Just then an officer in a peaked cap came round to Peter's window to inspect their two passports. Clemency could see the cogs turning in his mind. Two English diplomats. Not the same surname. Travelling together with skis on the roof for the weekend. Well, adultery was not a crime that concerned the French customs service.

'*Monsieur… mademoiselle…*'

He handed pack their passports and waved them on. No need to take their luggage into the shed to be checked. They were into France.

◊

Now that winter had come, St Quentin was like every ski holiday poster that Clemency had ever seen: the deep blue sky, the impossibly white mountains, the village nestling in the valley under a heavy blanket of snow, and even the brave little red-painted cable cars climbing the side of the mountain.

'It's a bit off the beaten track, but you can go over the col to Meribel and even as far as Courcheval if you want. It's the best of both worlds.'

Peter had pulled over to the side of the road so she could admire it, and she didn't disappoint.

'Oh, Peter, it looks wonderful! I know we're here for work but…'

'Don't worry about that. We're here for four nights, and the hand-over won't take more than an hour. The important thing is that we look like skiers enjoying ourselves, so that's what we must do.'

'Could we go out this afternoon?'

'Of course. We'll settle ourselves in. But first there's something we need to do in the village.'

◊

A few heads turned to follow her progress as she approached the foot of the cable car. And even a few heads was gratifying, for this was St Quentin, where the more discreet of the rich and the beautiful came to ski and to be seen. With little money and no pretentions to beauty, Clemency was unused to such attentions.

It was the coat.

Strolling along the single street of shops in St Quentin, she had fallen in love with it at first sight. Thick quilted kapok, tucked in at the waist to avoid too bulky a silhouette. Fleece lining and a mandarin collar than was just asking to have your head drawn down into it. Yet the price was impossible: ninety swiss francs – more than a week's salary.

And Peter had seen, and known, and offered to buy it for her.

They had argued, of course: it was far too much; it wasn't right; but he had been very persuasive, telling her that it was essential for the success of their mission that she looked the part, and her old coat was simply not St Quentin. Logic had served the purposes of temptation, and she had yielded. Once or twice, walking back to the chalet, she had wondered what else she had decided to yield; or he would expect her to yield.

Maybe it was not only the coat that made people look twice. They saw her new-found confidence. They responded to her knowledge that she was admired and desired. That a man like Peter Aspinal would risk his life for her. Passing Staněk to the Swiss hadn't been an afterthought. At least part of the reason why he had gone over the border was to rid her of the threat of the ruthless Da Silva.

Peter was waiting for her by the news-stand, idly turning the pages of a German motoring magazine. He smiled in welcome, and in appreciation of how much difference his impulsive gift had made.

'Ready? Then let's ski.'

◊

He was as good as she had expected. He knew the slopes well, too; taking her up on the cable car to the Pic de Lune, and down a blue run that snaked between the trees all the way back to the village, nearly seven miles with hardly another soul on the *piste*. The snow was crisp, resistant, so that she felt more confident in the turns, and pushed herself a little harder, a little further than she would ordinarily have gone, to keep up; and though clearly he was holding back, it didn't feel as if she were a burden to him.

He pulled up above the final slope down to the village.

'You're better than you made out,' he said, his breath clouding in the cold air. His face was flushed, his teeth very white.

'I'd forgotten how lovely it is in the mountains,' she replied.

'Did I tell you about Zuidwall? It's the newest of the mountain-top cafés. You get a good view of it from here.'

She followed the line of his outstretched arm. Across the shoulder of the nearest mountain was another valley and beyond that a peak topped by a low, round building whose rows of windows glinted in the sun. She could just make out the pylons of a cable car reaching up to it, and to the left, flanked by pines, were ski runs.

'It looks like a spaceship,' she said.

'Impressive, isn't it? There's a restaurant and a café, and then you can either ski back down to St Quentin or into the next valley. The view in the restaurant is amazing. Then there's a lower terrace on the other side, next to the cable car. That's where the café is.'

'Are we going to go there?'

'We are. Tomorrow afternoon. That's where the pick-up will be.'

'Oh.'

'Don't think about it. It will be a cinch. Now, let's see just how good you are. I'll race you to the bottom.'

He slowed towards the end, so she could have the pleasure of beating him in front of the small audience seated on the terrace of the café. She turned to wait for him, pushing up her goggles and smiling broadly.

'You let me win.'

'Not at all. I just had to slow down to admire you from behind.'

Peter found them a table and ordered their drinks, then excused himself to make a call. There was a payphone in a corridor towards the back of the restaurant – not very secure, but he only needed to listen, not to say much.

He was lucky; it only took a few minutes for the operator to connect his call; and there, in faraway London, he was talking to Swan's assistant, Roberts.

'It's Jeremy Harrison. Anything for me?'

'Nothing. You?'

'Nothing. I'll call same time tomorrow. Cheerio.'

He hung up. It was a ritual without much meaning. If there had been a problem, if he didn't phone in for one of the daily contacts, they'd assume that something had come up, or the lines were down, or that he'd got bored of waiting for his call to be put through. There would be no rescue mission.

In his absence, Clemency had been drawn into a group of young people at the next table. They were chattering away in French, much too fast and too colloquial for Peter. But, as they said, a picture was worth a thousand words; and the picture was of these boys flirting, and Clemency not minding that much.

He felt a pang of jealousy. She was that little bit more animated, more... he had to admit it, more relaxed with them, as they talked about bars or music or films or whatever. And she fitted in with these golden youths because, he saw afresh, she was rather lovely herself, with her face and figure and her character, her obvious desire to be pleased by those around her, to want to have fun, to think the best of everything and everyone.

But there was compensation for him; for as he joined the group, he remembered that it was he who was her companion, and these young bucks were deferring to him with what passed for the youth of today with respect.

One in particular; a boy of maybe twenty, his fair hair swept back, and an aristocratic nose, and fine cheekbones that had caught the sun a little, and that took the edge off the perfection of his profile and somehow made him all the more charming. He was leaning back in his chair, broad shoulders in his heavy sweater, and keeping his gaze fixed on Clemency, though he was aware of Peter's scrutiny. Probably Venetian, Peter thought; no other people could combine that fair complexion and that languid fluidity. He would be every shop-girl's dream of an Italian aristocrat; and he was setting out to please Clemency; and yet it was Peter that she turned to.

'Shall we head back to the village?'

◊

They took the last leg of their route at a steady pace. Clemency's muscles were starting to protest at the unfamiliar exercise, and she was thinking more and more of a hot bath before supper. But it had been a wonderful day and it seemed wrong not to acknowledge it. Peter had gone a little ahead, almost out of sight, and she was following his tracks. But around the next shoulder of the hill, he was waiting for her, and she made a creditable snowplough stop at his side.

'Everything OK?' he asked.

'Much better than that.'

He looked at her enquiringly, and though she knew she was gushing, she had to go on.

'You've been so good to me, Peter. I don't mean just the coat, though it is absolutely gorgeous. I mean letting me into your world. I've wanted to say this for a while, but it was never the right time. And in case it never is, I'm going to say it now.'

He stared down at her. What was this announcement? That she loved him? That she thought he loved her, she was sorry but It Could Never Be.

'Peter, you've given me a glimpse of a life I thought I'd only ever see at the cinema. I can see how much it demands of you. I don't mean only the danger. I mean putting yourself apart from the rest of the world. Wrapping yourself up in lies and deception. You're doing it because it needs to be done. No-one's going to thank you for it. If you ran into a burning building and pulled out a child, you'd be a hero. But what you're doing is secret. So if no-one else can thank you, I can.'

He cleared his throat.

'That was quite a speech. I don't know that I deserve it, but thank you.'

My God, he thought: *she's in love. She may not even realise it herself yet, but she is completely, desperately, tearing-her-apart-inside in love with me.*

What the hell do I do now?

It was flattering, of course. Here was a good-looking girl with brains, charm, who could have the pick of the young men in her life, and she'd plumped for him. But dangerous, too: if it were true that every woman loved with absolute abandon once in her life, then maybe, for her, this was it. This couldn't be a pleasant *affaire,* fun while it lasts and no regrets when it was over. If he tried that, she'd be devastated. There would

be scenes, recriminations, consequences. And beyond
even that – and the last thing he wanted was trouble at
the Embassy, perhaps having to return to London, with
a blot on his personnel file – he couldn't bring himself
to hurt her like that. The same passion burning inside
her – as she looked up at him, her eyes were bright, her
cheeks glowing, even her lips parted as if to help let the
heat within to escape – left her supremely vulnerable.

Without quite knowing how, she was in his arms, her
body warm and solid against his; and yet the fragility
was there too, the brittleness. Like a bulb, she was
burning so bright that she might burst at any moment.

He needed to think. A voice in his head was telling
him to step back, release her, and begin to rebuild the
walls between them – age, professionalism and the
rest. He needed to be the one to say It Could Never Be,
for she was beyond any such thoughts.

But there were other voices. One hardly needed to
find words – it was the simple urge to take her there
and then. But he was also asking himself if perhaps
this was his chance for something more permanent
than the long line of pleasant *affaires* stretching back
down the years. Had he ever planned to find himself
a wife, Clemency White would never have made the
shortlist. But perhaps his instincts were telling him
something about her inner qualities, or how she might
complement his own strengths.

Only one thing was certain.

'Clemency,' he whispered into her hair. 'We need to
wait one more day.'

Once the words were spoken, he realised they were
a commitment as well as a way to buy time. She had
stiffened, realising what this meant. Now she was
searching his face to see if it were true. She seemed

almost frightened: the kind of look she might have at the top of a ski jump or facing her first trip down the bobsleigh run; fear and anticipation mixed up with the almost sensual feeling of being alive and proving it by facing up to death.

'Tomorrow.'

She said it as a statement; a commitment. He wondered how she pictured it. Drinks, dinner, chat, touching, then the slow, gentle undressing and love-making before the fire? Or was her imagination different? More urgent? Returning from the slopes, hardly able to open the door to the chalet before tearing off each other's clothes, left strewn in a careless line from door to bed.

Well, he would find out soon enough.

'Tomorrow.'

◊

He'd assumed they would eat out for all their meals, but Clemency – in an unexpected moment of domesticity – had insisted she would prepare a goulash for them. She went off to the shops, string bag on her arm, and he lay back on the sofa and reviewed his preparations for the next day.

He awoke with a start as the door flew open. It was Clemency, flushed and out of breath, the shopping bag dumped unheeded on the floor.

'The man who came up to me in the street,' she said. 'You and Mr Dansby-Gregg asked me about him. I saw him. Or at least I think I did.'

'Where?' Now he was alert, on his feet, glancing to the drawer of the desk where his gun lay.

'In a car. Passing by when I was coming back from

the shop. It was only for a moment but I'm sure it was him.'

Peter frowned. It wasn't at all likely that Petrov would be operating in France. But if he was…

He wanted time to think. But not with Clemency there. She'd brought him this problem and was now standing there with that infuriating look of complete trust that he would know the answer.

'What car was it?'

'A Mercedes. Four doors. Dark green. A local number-plate.'

A 190. Or maybe a 110. Either way, it was the car he'd choose for an operation in the mountains. Plenty of power for the hills, and robust for the icy roads.

'Which way was it heading?'

'Down to the square, I think.'

'OK. Could you go to the café and pick me up some cigarettes. If you see the car, fine, but don't make it look like you're searching for it. And don't do anything silly like following him. Just come straight back.'

She nodded, serious and excited, and headed off. He waited until she was half-running down the slope back into town, picking her way nimbly between the ruts in the ice, and then breathed out.

Petrov? Here?

Was the tape more valuable than they thought? He'd had the impression from Petrescu that this was a sample of their merchandise, not the crown jewels. Would the Soviets set up a whole operation in a Western country to get it back? It would have to be on a massive scale – surveillance, a safe house, a trained Moscow team of watchers plus some local criminals to make up the numbers. They'd only do that if they had a strong source. A plant within the group of conspirators? It was possible – but then why let the thing go ahead, if they knew all about it. Much easier to liquidate them all back in Bucharest. If the tape as worth that much to them, why take the risk of letting it out of the country?

Coincidence? Was Petrov here for the skiing? He could put that out of his mind.

But he might be here to watch over Peter and Clemency, if he thought they were having an affair, if he thought there was the chance of blackmail. Say he knew where they were staying. Perhaps he had a tap on Peter's home phone. He could have turned up as a man from the electricity company and rigged up some camera or microphone to gather evidence of their illicit lovemaking. Maybe he thought this would be enough to blackmail Clemency into parting with some confidential material. It would be a much more simple job. Petrov and a technician was all they'd need.

No. Clemency might be mortified to receive those kinds of photos through the post, with the threat of them finding their way to the Ambassador; but she wasn't such a simpleton – or so disloyal – as to lead her to betray her country. That was one advantage of the modern girls, the Chelsea set: they were less traditional, less concerned about respectability than their mothers. But would Petrov know that?

Then there was the third explanation. Clemency had been spooked by being approached by Petrov in Bern. She'd taken a dislike to him. Perhaps she'd brooded on it. Telling her about the Czech cypher clerk had probably been a mistake. And Clemency was eager to please, to show she was pulling her weight, was a real help, not just there to look decorative.

Put the two together, and she'd seen a face in a car window – and there was nothing remarkable about

Petrov, to look at, a plain face behind the heavy black-framed glasses – and imagined the rest.

Those were the explanations. What were his options? Call it off? Try and set up the hand-over in another time and place, and hope it was third time lucky?

Or call London for reinforcements? He didn't like the sound of that. Could Swan get anyone out here in less than twenty-four hours? And they'd need to inform the Paris station, and probably the DST as well, and that would be embarrassing because they had an understanding not to mount these kinds of operations in each other's territories. He'd cause a flap, and they'd probably still have to call the thing off.

All on a face glimpsed in a passing car.

Should he call in one of his own goons from Bern? There was Franz Toller. And André, whom he'd used as back-up in a tricky move on a Hungarian diplomat working at the ILO. André was good with a knife. But both of them would look like fish flapping on the quayside in St Quentin. If they would come, at such short notice.

But in a way, the answer was simple. The original plan was right. And he'd devised it to cover exactly this possibility – that they might be jumped by the GRU. It's why the hand-over was in public, in the open; why they had a chalet, set back in its own quarter-acre of grounds, difficult to keep watch on, and not a hotel room, so there was no need to be hanging around waiting for a bill if they needed to move on in a hurry; why he'd spent two days exploring every side road and forest track between here and the border.

All the bases were covered, as the Americans would say.

It was good Clemency had come to him. Even if she were mistaken – and he was more and more convinced she was – it was a good bit of work. She'd even known the number plate was local. A smart girl.

It did no harm to be given a poke, he thought, as he found his coat, put on his boots, and readied himself to go and find her. Kept you sharp. No harm done, except that Clemency had needed to walk into the village twice.

But even then, it meant he'd have a spare packet of cigarettes.

16

The cable car sank as it left the lower station and passed over a stream and then a field where some cows were picking at bundles of hay. Then they began to rise, but sluggishly, and it looked as if they would not clear the pine-clad cliff rapidly approaching. But like an overladen plane reluctantly taking off, they finally gained some height, skimmed the trees, and rattled beneath the first of the towers that held the cables aloft. Clemency breathed out.

'Dramatic, isn't it?' Peter said in her ear. 'And the place we're going is another 1,500 feet up. I believe the view is quite something.'

It was the afternoon and there were only a handful of passengers, so it was easy for Clemency to look out over the valley to their left, look back to the cable car station, already becoming lost in the background clutter of the village.

'The shortest ski run is ten kilometres, but we'll come back via the wolf path. That's sixteen, but it's that bit easier.'

'Sixteen kilometres? I've never skied that far before.'

'You'll be fine. It's very clearly marked. And I'll be with you.'

Usually she liked the way he trusted her and believed she could do things she herself had never dreamed of. But sometimes it was disconcerting.

They were passing over a ski run now, filled with brightly coloured figures buzzing down the grey-white slope. Peter was right. It wasn't that far. There would be people around and she'd done much more skiing than that in a day, even if not on a single run.

Even if she had reservations, she couldn't say anything here, not with the other passengers so close. There were six of them, two dark-haired men, so similar they might have been brothers, who occasionally exchanged clipped sentences in Italian; two couples, neither of whom said anything at all. Maybe it was being in a cable car. There was a kind of compulsion in listening to the rumble of the wheels on the cable, seeking constant reassurance that all was well, sensitive to any change in tone, so that the woman nearest to her, gazing out of the window with the bored air of an experienced skier, still jumped a little when the rattled past the next pylon.

Were they being followed? Could one of them be a Soviet agent? Apart from the Italians, you couldn't tell their nationality. Not from the thick padded jackets and ski pants, the scarfs and gloves and the boots, the international costume of the skier. Not from their expressions, either. They weren't the usual chatting tourists; they were more serious skiers, or they took themselves more seriously.

'And there's the restaurant.'

She turned back to see where their destination had come into view. It was like nothing she had seen before. Perhaps the closest was the control tower of a modern airport, circular with the ring of large windows. It sat on the very peak, the walls built up from the rock in solid blocks of concrete. There were a few figures to be seen on the terrace below the restaurant, chatting in groups, pointing to the surrounding peaks, or watching the cable-car as it approached.

'I think we have time for a drink before we set off,' Peter announced, and she wondered if this was for the benefit of their fellow-passengers.

'I'd like that,' she said. 'Something hot.'

The cable-car arrived with a final clank and swing and the doors opened. They filed onto the platform, then up some stairs to a kind of cloak-room where they could leave their skis. Then they passed through glass doors into a cafeteria, with a serving area to one side and thirty or more tables filling the rest of the room. It was more utilitarian than she had expected. The floor was concrete with lino paint, and the tables were Formica.

She found a table by the long line of windows and Peter went to fetch their drinks, returning with a tray with two mugs, one piled with whipped cream.

'Hot chocolate for you. Set you up for the run back.'

She sipped the drink; looked up to find Peter laughing at her; then realised she had a blob of cream on her nose. But there was something a little forced about his smile; and his eyes were roaming around the room. She did the same; a dozen people scattered about in small groups, no-one on their own; no-one who looked out of place.

'Tell me about where you grew up,' he asked unexpectedly. 'Who are your people? Where did you go on your hols? That kind of thing.'

She was surprised; then realised that for them not to be talking would be suspicious.

'Well, where do I start? I was born in Dorchester. My father's a surgeon at the hospital there. Mummy was a nurse before they married. I have an older brother. He's a pilot with Caledonian Airways and lives in Glasgow, so I don't see as much of him as I would like. I had a very typical childhood, I expect. I wanted a pony but never got one. I wanted to be a dancer and I had the lessons, but I'm just a bit too tall. I loved school. It was a boarding school, and lots of outdoor things to do as well as studying. Swimming, gym, running. The headmistress believed that girls could do anything, which was a lovely thing to be told when you're young. And maybe it's true. When I was in the third form, there was a girl in the sixth who went to Cambridge to read physics; and a girl from my year has nearly finished training to be a doctor.'

'And you are here.'

'I suppose I could have gone to university. But more than anything I wanted to get away from England. I worked in London for a bit, then had a year as an *au pair* in Paris, and that was wonderful. Then some work for a travel company, and I picked up some Spanish and some Italian. I took Russian A level, and though I couldn't go there, obviously, I made sure I listened to Radio Moscow for a couple of hours each week.'

He looked so shocked that she began to sing *Wide is my Motherland*, the patriotic tune they played at the start of each hour on Radio Moscow. He was about to tell her to shut up, when he realised she was being more natural than he was. If anyone were following them, hearing her sing a Russian song would tell them precisely nothing.

'What about you?' she asked. 'You must have a more interesting tale to tell then me. After all, you've lived a lot longer,' she added, her eyes wide with false innocence.

Still there was no sign of the contact, so Peter chatted on with half his mind about growing up during the war, joining up just in time for the last months, his role in the anti-insurgency plans for the newly-occupied German territories – the insurgency that thankfully never amounted to much.

'To tell the truth, my war never really got going. Maybe that's why I was tempted to stay in when everyone else was desperate to get out and go home.'

He talked a bit about some of his postings, Berlin and Saigon and Hong Kong, though not what he'd done there; and then about his plans for stepping back from working in the field.

'Time for me to fly a desk for a bit, take it easy, stop living on my nerves. Settle down a bit. It's not a life for life, if you see what I mean.'

'Will you be leaving soon?' she asked, trying not to sound disappointed.

'Oh no, it's just something I'm mulling over.'

Beyond the windows, the valley was now completely in shadow, and the sun on the upper slopes was taking on the reddish tinge of the late afternoon. The café was emptying, as the skiers made their final descent of the day. Still no contact.

Peter was on edge, however much he tried to hide it. He leaned forward, speaking low.

'Don't turn around, but there are two goons at the table behind the pillar.'

'How can you tell?'

'Little things. Too watchful. Lingering over their coffees. And their ski wear is badly cut and out of date in a way that only manufacturers behind the Iron Curtain can manage.'

'They'll see the hand-over. If he still comes.'

'Yes, and there might be some rough stuff too. Look, you'd better go. It's no good thinking there's any hope of fooling them that we're just another couple. And if there is any trouble, I don't want to have to worry about you.'

She began to protest, but he insisted.

'Clemency, there's no time to argue. It's an order.'

She nodded.

'So, in a minute or two, tell me you're going back to the village, drink up, kiss me goodbye and take yourself off. It's just possible that they'll have another couple of watchers on the main run, so choose one of the other routes. I'll meet you in the *Friedrichszellar* at seven o'clock. If I'm not there by eight, go up to the hotel and call a taxi down to the station at Chambéry. You'll be in time for the last train to Geneva tonight. I want you on it. Don't wait for me. Don't go back to the chalet. Understand? I'll be fine, but this may need to be a lone game.'

'Take care of yourself,' she said quietly.

'Don't worry,' he grinned. 'You and I have some unfinished business.'

He watched her as she crossed the café, moving so gracefully, the bulky coat making her seem all the more slim and attractive underneath.

Once the door had swung shut behind her, he turned his mind back to the job. It was all very well awarding himself the prize, but he had to earn it first.

He glanced at his watch. It was nearly four o'clock. Either they weren't coming, or they had spotted the goons as well and were waiting for Peter to make a move, to open up the board, let them get near him.

He went over to the servery, where a bored girl was filing her nails, waiting for the place to shut. He bought a newspaper and a bar of chocolate he didn't really want, then went onto the terrace outside. He found a spot in the sun, and began to leaf through the paper. He was glad he'd got Clemency out of this situation – he had a bad feeling about it – but it meant he looked very conspicuous on his own. Who would actually come to the top of a mountain to read a paper?

He went to fetch his skis from the cloakroom. Here was a more convincing way to burn a few minutes. He took them to the balcony beside the entrance to the cable-car station and began to fiddle with the bindings, adjusting them, then checking that his boots still fitted just the way he wanted them to.

Five minutes; still nothing.

He left the skis standing there and crossed to the entrance to the toilets. His boots skittered on the tiled floor and for a second he thought he was going to slip. A man coming out smiled at him briefly in sympathy. He went to one of the urinals and stood there, relieved himself, went and washed his hands until to do so any longer would start to look odd. But there was no-one there to see. He was glad, because the toilets had no second way out, and he didn't like the idea of he and his contact being cornered there.

He came back into the daylight. There was really nothing else to do but to go. The goons were still there, sitting blank-faced over their empty coffee cups. The silent couple from the cable-car were gone. Staying any longer was all risk and no reward.

He passed round the base of the building to the beginning of the ski runs. There was a large signboard that showed the different routes, with their length, their difficulty, and their final destination. He should have told Clemency which one to take. She was not much more than twenty minutes ahead, and he could probably still catch her up. Not the black run. Maybe the green? It was the easiest. Or the brown? That was the one most people took, who didn't think of themselves as crack skiers. But there was also the blue, the violet, the pink. He frowned.

They would meet back at the bar. It didn't matter.

'Please stay exactly where you are.'

The words were spoken quietly from behind. For a moment, he thought of resisting. But then again, there was the barrel of a gun resting against the base of his spine.

'Of course,' he said calmly. 'How can I help?'

◊

Clemency had acted out the little play he had sketched out for her, then gone to the washroom before collecting her skis. The attendant eyed her sourly as she paid her ten *centimes*, as if put out that she could not shut up and go home. And certainly there was little custom to be had. Clemency was alone except for a middle-aged woman with harshly dyed blonde hair, adjusting her bobble hat in one of the mirrors.

'Your coat… I like it very much,' she said to Clemency in stilted English. 'May I?'

She touched the fabric; but the look she gave Clemency was filled with meaning, and in a brief moment she had slipped a package into her pocket. With a slight nod, she was gone, leaving Clemency still standing at the basin, thinking furiously. She couldn't go back to Peter, however much she wanted to; all she could do was follow his instructions. Perhaps he had expected this; that it was obvious to this agent that she and Peter were being observed, and the exchange would have to take place where the watchers could not see them. She slid the package inside her jacket. It was something flat, circular, light: a roll of film from a projector, perhaps. She buttoned up her coat to the top, adjusted her scarf and left.

Even the gaze of the attendant now seemed sinister. Would the watchers realise what had happened? She collected her skis, came round to the front of the building, glanced briefly at the map, picked a route almost at random, then stepped into her skis and fixed the bindings in place.

Then, suddenly, it was all right. She was on her way, gaining speed, gaining confidence too, as picked up the first of the violet marker posts that would guide her down to the village. Sixteen kilometres. Less than an hour full out; but she was going to take it easy. She had no intention of having a fall, not skiing alone, not towards the end of the day when it might be a long time before another skier came past to help her.

She came to a fork in the *piste;* most of the other routes went off to the left, but violet and pink went to the right. Soon she was skiing between the first of the pines, just able to survive at this height, but stunted by the harsh conditions. The snow was firm, crisp, ideal conditions, and she was enjoying herself; even more so when she thought of Peter's expression when he met her at the bar, and he didn't have the package, and she could oh-so-casually slide it across the table to him.

The slope was a little steeper, and she built up some extra speed, the breeze icy but refreshing, no match for the thickness of her coat, the sense of progress delightful. She wanted to sing. Why not? There was no-one else around.

There was something magical about being alone on the mountainside, evening approaching, the frost starting to crisp up the surface of the snow, so that the sound of the skis took on a sharper, rougher sound against the background of absolute silence. No breeze in the trees, no voices, not even a bird singing.

She passed through another stand of pines, and then the *piste* opened out again. She recognised the outcrop of rock that broke through the snow away to her right. An old friend, she had dozed in its shade. This was the very meadow where they had picnicked the summer before. She came to a halt, looking about and wondering at the transformation of the alpine pasture where the villagers would bring their cattle in the spring, camping out for weeks on end, to take advantage of the sweet lush grass, now hidden under a mantle of perfect snow.

She too was so different; the Clemency of the summer would not have been carrying a secret tape or be wondering if she would be sleeping with a colleague that evening.

Then something made her turn.

High above her on the slope were two figures; two men approaching at speed, hunched over, poles tucked in. And they were making straight for her.

She dug her poles in and pushed off, but was sure they would catch her long before she reached the safety of the village. How stupid of her not to think of it. Already they were in calling distance.

'Mam'zelle! Attention! Arrêtez-vous!'

She glanced back. They were much closer, waving their arms in warning.

'This path is closed. There is danger ahead.'

She snowploughed to a halt and waited for them to come up, almost laughing in relief. They were French, and were no doubt knew a hundred times more about the mountains and its dangers than she did.

'Is there another way down?' she called back as they approached.

'Yes, yes, we will show you. It is lucky for you that we came, though.'

They draw to a halt in a little, flashy flurry of snow, both very experienced on ski. They were puffing and smiling, and after the loneliness of the run down the mountain she realised how grateful she would be for their company. And it was only as she began to wonder how long the diversion would take, and whether she would be late for her meeting with Peter, that one of them drew out a short, heavy piece of pipe wrapped in cloth and smashed it against the back of her head.

17

She woke into a world of confusion. Everything was blinding, blue and white, unbelievably cold. She tried to move, and the sky and the clouds and the snow danced and span. The one constant was the pulsing pain at the back of her head. She explored with her fingers, and they came away sticky with blood, matted into her hair, red against the white of the snow.

Fear returned, and she looked about her; but the men were gone.

So too was her coat. She sat up, but there was no sign of it anywhere. They must have stolen it, she thought; and somehow this made her angrier than being attacked. Her beautiful coat. And how she wanted it. Her thin sweater was little use against the biting chill of the mountainside. And much as she wanted to rest, and recover, she rose shakily to her feet.

One ski lay nearby, as if she had simply taken a tumble on the slope; but of the other, there was no sign; and even the one she had was useless. The bindings had been torn way, so there was no way to attach the ski to her boot.

She looked about her, anxious to see some other skiers, or a mountain guide or shepherd, or anyone who could come to her aid. But the valley was empty. Just rank upon rank of dark pine trees rising on either side, and the snow-clad slope between which followed the line of a hidden stream.

There was nothing else for it but to make her own way down from the mountain. And she would need to hurry.

Even as she stood there, the lengthening shadows were reaching towards her. At once, it felt bleak as well as freezing cold. She shivered more than ever and wrapped her arms around herself, then tried beating them against her sides, rubbing them down her legs, anything to warm herself and get the blood flowing back. How long had she lain there unconscious? The cold had seeped deep into her, and she would need every ounce of warmth if she were going to make it.

It was natural to follow the tracks that the two men had left, running like tram-lines into the distance; and in any case, there was no alternative. She was closer to the village than to the head of the mountain, where the cable-car and the café stood; and walking uphill would take an age. She began to plod down the slope, each step sinking deep into the virgin snow.

She tried not to think of the package. It was no good telling herself it was bad luck, or that Peter should never have involved her. If she had been more awake, she wouldn't have let them get near her; would never have stopped when they called.

She was shivering uncontrollably. It was at least five miles back to the village. She guessed she was doing little more than a mile an hour, and it was going to be a long night. When she glanced behind her, it was sickening to see how little distance she had covered.

For a while, she occupied her mind by considering what she would buy to replace the coat they had stolen and wondering if she would ever be truly warm again. Her hands were literally blue, her face numb, and she tried to recall something she had once read about frostbite.

Then she stepped into an unexpectedly deep drift, stumbled forward, and was left on her hands and knees, head drooping, unable for a moment to summon up the energy to stand once more. Wading through the snow was sapping her strength every bit as quickly as the cold.

Only now did she realise that they hadn't stolen her coat, as if they were common thieves. That was absurd. They had taken it so that she would die out here; die of exposure. It was the same with her skis; tearing off the bindings from one, and hiding the other, so that she would have to walk.

It was a much better way to kill her than a knife. Just another regrettable skiing accident; another young girl without enough sense to stay with others, who must have left her coat at the top of the mountain and relied on getting back to the village before the sun set.

She stumbled on in the half-darkness, more slowly now, her mind drifting away from the terror of the present to the time she had come here the last summer, to these same mountains. Then, it had been a picture-book Alpine pasture, all flowers and sunshine and droning bees. There had been meat-paste sandwiches and flasks of tea, just as if they had been in a meadow in England. Warm, drowsy, like brandy; like Clemency was starting to feel now.

She had spent much of the time gossiping with Mrs Dansby-Gregg, very grand, for all she was not much older than Clemency, but also good fun, because she was capable of saying anything, and had the beauty and the style to carry it off. Before the picnic, the opinion of the clerks' room was that Mrs Dansby-Gregg was half-mad and would in time become either a dipsomaniac or a nymphomaniac, or perhaps both; but by the time they returned to Bern, Clemency had decided she was simply bored beyond belief. And who could blame her, married to Cedric Dansby-Gregg.

'A terrible dry old stick. Imagine going to bed with him!'

Who had spoken? It was hard to think; hard to do anything but sink to her knees.

I'm going to die, she told herself. No more picnics. No more skiing. No parties or dances or flirting. No future. No husband, no children. No letting herself be undressed by Peter in front of the flickering fire.

She found that anger was the last source of resolve. Everything else faded away, leaving only the desire to reappear in the village, and face up to the men who had taken her coat and ruined her skis and left her to perish alone on the mountainside.

But she couldn't make it back to the village. She had gone no more than a mile, and she was finished, and there were four more miles to go.

But there was the hut, the one Mrs Dansby-Gregg had told her about, lying in the warm grass and trying to shock Clemency by recommending it as a safe place to go when she had decided with which of the diplomats she was going to have an affair; and seemingly not leaving her husband out of contention.

'Follow the path along the stream,' she had said in her dreamy, cultured voice. 'You'll come to a tree with a face in it. A real face. Or rather, it's a natural feature that someone has carved into a face. With a long beard and staring eyes. Just there, you turn left up another track and the cabin's no more than ten minutes. No-one ever goes there. It has candles, and blankets, and a lock on the door if you care about that sort of thing.'

Clemency pulled herself to her feet.

◊

It was nearly dark when she found the face on the tree; so nearly dark that she almost missed it; that she had to run her fingers over it to convince herself it wasn't a trick of the fading light; that some unknown artist with a knife and a surprising amount of talent had turned the natural features into those of a face; a haunting one, because it kept some of the spirit of the tree, and was wild, perhaps implacable.

Now she could pick up the path; because there was little snow under the trees, and it showed up pale against the masses of pine needles to each side. She plodded on for minutes, hours, it was impossible to tell; and at last there was the hut, in a half-clearing, grey against the darker mass of the trees behind.

Shelter. Maybe a blanket, maybe a fire or even something to eat. She would survive, and in the morning, when she was warm, and she could see where she was going, she would walk down to the village and find Peter. And he would look after her.

Then she stopped dead. There was a light inside; voices; and after the men who had tricked her on the slopes, she would never trust anyone ever again.

18

Peter was bored. Bored of blaming himself for the loss of the tape, and for what would happen to the conspirators back in Romania, with the GRU hours away from identifying them and lining them up for arrest, torture and disposal. He was bored of the pain, the sitting tied to a chair while they waited for the return of Petrov and the rest of the party, who had gone to arrange his transport away from the mountain and presumably back to Moscow or on to Siberia. And he was bored of cursing himself for a stupid, arrogant, careless fool.

How had they done it? They had the tape, so they must have spotted and jumped the courier. The only consolation was the Clemency was out of it.

The Russian, Temnikov, was young for a GRU officer, perhaps no more than twenty-five, and was keyed up, conscious of the responsibility Petrov had left him with. Making a show of being relaxed, he'd found a pack of cards and was playing patience, with his gun and the package with the tape in it lying to hand on the table. But he was tensed, listening intently, and every few seconds his eyes flickered to where Peter was sitting, and to where the guard sat watching.

Taking his cue from Temnikov, the guard too had laid down his gun; as it to show that Peter, bound to his chair, was no threat whatsoever. Georges, they had called him; probably a local French hoodlum borrowed for the occasion, in his forties, heavy-set, a scarred face. He might not have Temnikov's intelligence, but there was plenty of cunning and awareness in his steady gaze.

And he would follow orders – to hurt, to kill – because the money would be right.

Peter refused to think what would happen when he was on the other side of the Iron Curtain. In the end he would break. No-one could be expected to stand up to the torture – not so much the pain as the psychological effects of sleep deprivation, isolation, fear, and the doses of drugs, a combination that would in the end wear down his resistance, wash away each rampart of his defences like the tide lapping over a sandcastle. It was all about buying time for London to save what they could from his networks.

What was Petrov's plan? Peter thought through what he would do if the tables were turned. There was no way to bring a vehicle up to the hut. He wouldn't want to bring Peter down on foot, even with his four goons. It would always look odd to a casual passer-by, and Petrov would not want any witnesses. So, a sledge. Peter would be lashed to it, covered in blankets, they would get as far as the outskirts of the village that way, and then drive to their safe house. They were bound to have a base nearby; and they could wait there until they had a plan in place to get him out of the country.

Peter told himself there was always hope; maybe that was where his chance would come.

◊

The first thing Clemency found when she began to scout out the hut was an open woodshed at the back where the occupants had stacked their skis and poles and left some things they didn't need any more.

Including her coat.

She slipped it on, closing her eyes in anticipation of

the feeling of warmth it might one day bring; stuffing her hands deep into the pockets and there – joy – coming across a bar of chocolate. It was frozen solid, but she gnawed off a chunk and let it begin to dissolve in her mouth.

Then she risked a glance into one of the unshuttered windows. It was a storeroom of some kind that was being used as a kitchen, with a Primus stove and an oil lamp. Otherwise, it was empty. The window was open a crack for ventilation, but there was a lock in place and it wouldn't go up any further.

She crept to the next window. A man sat playing patience; a gun to one side. She ducked down again, but had taken in the rest of the room. Peter tied to the chair; another man watching him.

She sat crouched with her back against the wooden wall of the hut, trying to think. She should go for help; but even with her coat, it would take her hours, and maybe she wouldn't make it at all. And by the time she had found help – would there even be a police station in St Quentin? – and convinced them what was happening, Peter would have been spirited away.

Unless…

She went back to the wood store and examined the skis. They were much too long for her, but they would have to do. She took the shorter pair and worked at the clips, so that her own boots would fit in them.

She laid them out; and then thought again.

◊

Temnikov finished his game and came over to stand in front of Peter. He removed the gag that had been tied loosely across Peter's mouth.

'I suppose you are still an innocent English tourist who has no idea why he is here and demands to speak to the British consul?'

Temnikov was amused, but not gloating.

'I don't know who you are or what you want, but you've got the wrong man,' Peter replied.

'Yes, of course. But let us say that I am right, and you are an officer of the English secret service, then you will appreciate the situation. We have reclaimed the property of my authorities. We wish to return home with this property, without any difficulties or interference. Therefore, you must be held until that is complete. Then you will be free to go.'

'If you let me go now, I won't cause any trouble,' Peter insisted, still in his threadbare role of an innocent citizen. 'If you are spying on the French, that's not my affair.'

'How considerate of you. But as I said, if you are what I think you are, then I want you to continue to be the professional. As I do not want you to be stupid, I will explain—'

There was a crash from the kitchen; something falling, or a window breaking. Temnikov swung round. The guard yanked open the door. Flames were licking across the floor of the store room. There wasn't much smoke, and Peter could make out the remains of an oil lamp.

Temnikov seized a blanket and began to beat at the flames. The oil spread to the blanket, and he dropped it with a curse. It began to smoulder, but though there was more smoke, the flames were already dying down.

'Drop the gun.'

Clemency stood by the table, Petrov's gun in her hands. She was standing as Peter had taught her, feet apart, both hands on the gun, and she looked like she knew what she was doing. The guard crouched down and laid his gun on the floor.

'Kick it away.'

He did so, just as Temnikov snapped at him to wait.

'It's the girl from the café. She's not an agent. She's only a clerk.'

'A clerk with a gun,' she said. 'Get down onto the floor, face down. Both of you.'

The guard looked uncertain, but Temnikov began to walk slowly towards her.

'Don't be stupid,' he said quietly. 'Your boyfriend is in no danger. This is purely business.'

'Stay back.'

'Put down the gun before someone is hurt.'

As if in answer, she slipped the safety catch and fired into the ceiling.

But it was the wrong thing to do. Temnikov was already too close. He leapt forward and caught her hand as she brought the gun down.

She fired again.

He let go of her arm and slowly began to turn round, while Clemency stared at him, her face drained of blood.

Then Peter saw why. One of his eyes had gone. There was a little blood, almost black, in the socket.

Temnikov began to moan and then to blunder across the room from wall to wall, like a trapped fly.

'Merde,' the guard said. He looked to where his gun lay, but Clemency was there before him, ignoring Temnikov, pocketing the man's gun.

'Are there any others?' she asked. Her voice was like ice, and it took Peter a moment to realise she was talking to him.

'No. They went off about an hour ago. On skis. They won't be much longer.'

She pointed to the guard to get to the floor. Something in his expression, or perhaps the sight of Temnikov, now crouched rocking meaninglessly back and forth, left him helpless to resist. She slipped found a jack-knife in his pocket and cut Peter's bonds. He rubbed his freed wrists, stretched his cramped legs.

All the time, the animal sounds from Temnikov were scratching at his nerves. He wanted him to stop; to die. Peter had once driven over a cat and gone back to find it twitching and screaming in much the same way; and he'd had to silence it with the back of a snow shovel.

'There are two pairs of skis outside,' Clemency said. 'One should be OK with your boots. Where is your coat?'

It was, Peter thought, as if she were absolutely furious; the clipped sentences; the pinched white face with blotches of colour on her cheeks.

He thought: *she will never be the same again*.

He tied the guard up with what was left of the bindings. The man lay without moving, his eyes fixed on what remained of Temnikov. The fire she had started was almost out, the smoke starting to disperse. They went outside, retrieved the skis, and began to make their way down the path. Soon they were at the tree with the carved face, and the wide slope of the ski run was away to their left.

'Let's head over there,' he said quietly. 'We should see them coming, but we want to be well out of their way.'

'Yes.'

They went at a steady pace across the open space,

the route clear in the starlight reflecting from the snow. Apart from the hiss of their skis, there was no sound.

Soon Peter spotted one of the markers, and they kept just to the left of it, ready to break off into the woods if they were spotted. But there was no sign of the rest of Petrov's men.

After another kilometre, Clemency waved for him to stop. She drew out Temnikov's gun from her pocket.

'Please will you take this?'

Instinctively, he checked the safety catch and then slid it into his pocket. He wanted to comfort her, reassure her that she'd had no choice, that it had been the GRU man or her. But she had already set off again; and in any case, there was nothing he could say that could possibly help her.

19

Even with chains on the tyres, Peter's car struggled with the snow, now being picked up and driven by the rising wind. They had cleared out the chalet in five minutes and were now making for the border. With luck, the GRU would sort out their own mess, and there would be no need to involve the French authorities. But the car was built for the summer, and it was too close to the ground, so the ruts threatened to smash away the exhaust; and the windscreen wipers were struggling to push aside the heavy wet flakes; and the cold was coming through every gap.

He changed plans; took a side road away from the border, a route there was no reason to think they might be followed. In any case, the wind would soon cover their tracks. The going was a little easier, but he didn't want to use up his luck. A couple of times the rear of the little car slid away and they almost ended up in a ditch. That would be a disaster. He found a forest track and drove up far enough to be well out of sight of the road, backed the car between a couple of trees that would give some added shelter, and began to prepare to spend the night.

He'd picked up some bread and cheese and wine from the chalet. Clemency couldn't manage anything, but did consent to take a few sips of brandy from his hip flask. Then she let him lower the back of the passenger seat as far as it would go, tuck a blanket around her, and let her go off to sleep.

It was shock, he knew. With luck, by morning she

would be more herself. Not unchanged, but at least not this silent, wounded, far-away version of herself.

With the engine off, the car was getting cold. He pulled his cap over his ears, wiggled his toes, swigged a little more wine.

Odd, he thought; this was just the kind of romantic setting he might have used to seduce her – well, not exactly seduce, more help her go where he had no doubt she wanted to go. He had decided it was time, sitting in the café. And that time would come. Tomorrow they would cross the border, go back to the Embassy; he would file his report; and then he would take her back to his flat, and to his bed.

Looking at her, leaning against his shoulder, wrapped up to the nose in her coat and cap and blanket, she looked like a child; but he had never felt closer to her in age than now. She had grown up so very fast, he told himself. Those few moments in the hut were when her childhood ended and she became a woman.

They said that love and death were two sides of the same coin, he thought. Well, she had faced death tonight; and tomorrow, she would know love.

◊

He woke at first light, tired and stiff and chilled to the bone. He eased his joints and muscles one by one, trying not to wake Clemency, and began to plan the day. The opposition were probably a hundred miles away by now, Temnikov's body disposed of, the safe house closed down, the rest of the gang paid off. But he wasn't going to take any chances. They'd go further east, away from the mountains, with their narrow, lonely roads; down into the valley of the Rhône, taking the *départementales* from town to town, and work their cautious way up towards Mulhouse.

He'd call London for fresh instructions; either to head for a rendezvous with someone from the Paris station; or to make his own way back over the border to Bern. Coming from Mulhouse would mean entering Switzerland from the north, and it was inconceivable that the Soviets could cover all the borders, however much they wanted the tape. He turned the plan over in his mind, liking it more and more. The drive might be long and tiring for both of them, but it was safer. And it would give Clemency more time to come to terms with her ordeal.

He decided to set off there and then, in the half-light of the dawn. The heater would be welcome, and Clemency could go back to sleep, and the torture of thinking of coffee and warm rolls or croissants would abate a little. He got the car back on the road and set off for Chambéry. It was nearly a hundred miles, perhaps three hours, but they would make better time once they were on the RN90, and they could breakfast at Albertville.

The wind had dropped, and the road was in fair condition, and Peter contained his impatience and the undertone of anxiety that returned when he realised just how few cars were on the roads at this time of day. He had no intention of blundering into the GRU team, and there would not be many red MG sports cars around, despite the English passion for winter sports.

He'd explained his plan in a few words to Clemency, enough to get her to go back to sleep. She'd said little, but the shell-shocked look of the night before was gone, and he knew that, somehow, she was going to cope.

Soon they had reached the valley of the Isère, and

there was more traffic that both slowed their journey and gave them some cover. The last time Peter had driven this way it had been high summer, the tiny fields and orchards that lined the road brim-full with produce, the big farmhouses newly painted and prosperous. Now it was heavy cloud, ice, and the colours were drained out of everything, so that the red and white markers on the bends were startling bright.

He found a quiet backstreet in Albertville, and they strolled to a café in the main square. This was opposite the imposing bulk of the *PTT*, and as they waited for their breakfast to come, Peter was tempted to go over there and commit the tape to the French postal service, and let it make its own way back to London. It would be a weight off his mind; but a mix of duty, habit and the desire to bring the thing home himself stopped him.

Unconcerned by any such thoughts, Clemency was working her way that morning's *Le Dauphine Libéré*, which at least helped her to blend in, though travellers in ski wear were not infrequent in the Savoie.

'Encore deux café au lait,' he said to the waiter.

'You read my mind,' she said, not looking up from her paper, and it struck him that they were like a couple, not needing to make conversation, happy just to be together. What did that mean? Was he planning to marry her? Maybe he could do worse.

He could have sat there all morning, looking out over the square and planning his future; but they had a long way to go and so once they had finished their coffee he led her back to the car.

He quickly picked up the signs to Chambéry and settled down for the drive. He'd taken the Michelin map to the café and studied the route, so Clemency could go back to sleep. That was the best medicine – the sight of Temnikov stumbling around the hut, his brain pulped by the single bullet, had turned Peter's stomach, and he hated to think what Clemency was feeling inside.

How much should he share with London about what had happened in St Quentin? What would they make of the unvarnished truth? He'd got Clemency into that mess, and he felt the same responsibility he'd once felt for the soldiers under his command. If anyone was going to discipline them, it was him; and if they screwed up, he took the blame.

But as in any army, you didn't seek out trouble. Often, those above would rather have their reports cleaned up a little. He began to draft in his mind some of the more tricky passages. *At the rendezvous, the GRU appeared in force. He was briefly detained in a nearby forester's hut. Due to some carelessness on their part, he was able to escape, taking the tape with him.*

The only difficulty was Temnikov. As he'd said to Clemency long ago, one of the few rules of the game was that you didn't kill officers of the enemy service. Agents and hirelings didn't count, and had Clemency shot the French thug then there would have been no repercussions. But Temnikov's death might make life more dangerous for any of the Service's officers. He couldn't hold that information back.

A voice whispered to his inner self that they didn't know for sure that Temnikov was dead. But he had only to think of the man swaying, the uncanny sound he had made, the way he lay twitching on the floor, to know.

He would have to tell them; and could he really keep Clemency out of it?

These thoughts swirled around during the long drive up the Rhône valley. Better to be back in Bern when the balloon went up, Peter thought. And there was always the chance that the GRU had planned some kind of counter-stroke – perhaps a tip-off to the police.

Maybe the sooner they were back in Switzerland, under cover of diplomatic immunity, the better.

Another few minutes and they were coming into Mâcon, the Rhône broad and majestic to their right. Ahead was the bridge: straight on to Dijon, and perhaps to Paris; right over the bridge for the road to Bourg-en-Bresse and Geneva.

Three hours. That lovely straight road between Mâcon and Bourg. Even allowing for a stop for lunch, they would be in Switzerland well before dusk. By six, they could be back at the Embassy. A short telegram to London, put the tape in the diplomatic bag, and he and Clemency could be home by eight. Supper. And then…

Yes. And then.

He savoured the thought. The lights changed, and he turned onto the bridge, the exhaust bouncing from the old stone of the parapet, and they were heading back into the foothills of the Alps.

20

They were nearing the head of the pass, Peter gunning the engine, one hand off the wheel ready to change down as they neared the next hairpin bend.

And then the front tyre blew.

That should have been that. To the right was a low wall that would hardly have stopped a donkey and cart, and beyond that a sheer drop of five hundred feet down to the scree slopes of the Crêt de Péron. But there was no sanctuary to their left; only a sheer wall of living rock to throw them back across the road and into the void.

The car slewed across the road, the engine screaming. Clemency felt strangely calm; looked over to where Peter was fighting the steering wheel, dabbing the brake, using every ounce of skill and knowledge of the car.

They touched the low wall and she had a glimpse of the tops of stunted pines far below.

And then somehow they were slowing, and she almost had time to think they would make it unscathed before they drifted back across the road and smashed into the cliff.

A moment later, she lifted her head. There was pain across her chest where the seat belt had dug in. The window was crazed. Something had struck her forehead. A few drops of blood stained her sweater.

But she was alive. And Peter was alive; and even grinning.

'You won't believe me,' he croaked. 'But that was

one of my finest pieces of driving.'

She began to laugh.

◊

They sat on the low wall, their backs to the cliff edge that had so nearly claimed their lives. Without speaking, Peter pulled out his case, lit a cigarette, passed it to her and lit one for himself.

'Chance in a million,' he said.

'Escaping?'

'No, the blow-out. At that moment, right on the bend. Someone up there is looking after us.'

Instinctively, she glanced up at the side of the mountain, the piled-up jumble of rocks.

'I think I still have some brandy left.'

Carefully, not wanting to show any weakness, he stood and went back to the car, tried the boot. It sprung open with a nasty creak of rending pressed steel. But he soon had the flask in his hand. Then he paused. A car was approaching.

'That's a bit of luck.'

It was a Mercedes, dark green, French plates. The driver, seeing the smash, rolled to a halt and Peter went to provide the explanations and appeal for assistance, and the man in the passenger seat leant out of the window and trained a gun on him.

◊

They had the two of them lying on the tarmac while they searched the car. Four men; one of them she thought she recognised as one of her attackers from the slopes above St Quentin. There were two others in a similar mould; silent, watchful, and very comfortable with guns in their hands or with rifling through luggage; and Petrov. After a few moments, one of them pulled out a package. The tape.

Petrov unwrapped it and looked at the reel, though it was impossible to say if it meant anything to him. He slid it into his pocket and came over to Peter.

'You have caused a great deal of trouble,' he said. His English was slow, accented, but clear enough; as was the latent anger behind his expressionless face. 'This was to be routine. You have the tape. We take it from you. But now a man is dead. His blood is on your head.'

Peter had said they didn't kill unless absolutely necessary, but the mountainside was a very lonely place.

'Shall I tell you about him, Major Peter Aspinal of the English Secret Service? His name was Vassily Temnikov. He was twenty-three and this was his first assignment. I chose him because his father was a comrade of mine, many years ago, and Vassily is – was – like a nephew to me. That was the man, no, the boy that you shot.'

'He didn't shoot him,' Clemency said. 'I did.'

'Is this true?' he asked Peter.

'Of course not,' he replied.

Petrov stood and then gestured to one of the guards to come over. He kept his gun trained on Peter while he was tied and then bound so that hands and feet were locked together over his back. Only then did Petrov lift Clemency up and lead her over to the edge of the cliff.

'So you shot him?' he asked quietly.

She looked down into the valley. In a patch of green almost beneath her feet, some tiny white specks resolved themselves into a flock of sheep.

'Yes.'

His blow caught her on the side of the head and she fell sprawling to the ground. He stood over her.

'The boy is dead and he is not a subject of your stupid heroics. You think I am a fool? You think I want my time wasted in this way?'

She could hardly see for the pain, and her ear was ringing. She expected another blow; when it didn't come, she raised her head and saw that Petrov was listening. A car, approaching from the French side of the valley.

He grabbed her by the wrist and pulled her over to the remains of the MG; two of the guards picked Peter up and dropped him out of sight between the car and the rocks.

And at once the car was coming round the bend, slowing, and stopping. A Peugeot, modern and sleek, carefully tended, so that the chrome bumpers gleamed in the sunlight.

The man who leaned out of the window was in his early fifties, well-groomed, with dark hair and thick dark-framed glasses.

'Is there a problem?'

He spoke as if he thought it was just another car accident. But there was an edge of suspicion to his voice.

'Everything's fine,' the taller of the guards called back. 'There's no need for you to stop.'

But the man did stop. He climbed heavily from the car and came across, while his wife leaned across the empty driver's seat to see more of what was happening.

'Tell him everything is good,' Petrov whispered to Clemency.

The gun dug into her spine.

'Everything is fine,' she called out, her voice high and bright, but with a hint of desperation, like a host reassuring her guests that she did not need any help, when the kitchen was filled with smoke and the meal burnt to cinders.

The man stopped, puzzled. He put his hands on his hips, so that his jacket was pulled back and his stomach bulged out over the waistband of his trousers. Behind his thick glasses, he frowned.

'Should I call at the next garage for you?'

'There is no need,' the tall man said, his voice impatient. 'All is good.'

Still the man would not go away. Clemency had met the type before. He was a professional, a doctor or a businessman, and used to being in command, to the deference of those around him. Here, he sensed he was being lied to and he could not find a way to back off.

He took refuge in sudden action.

'You must move the cars from the road,' he announced, and walked briskly to the MG, as if to start pushing it to one side himself.

'No.'

But it was too late. Moving forward, he saw Peter lying there. He turned, his face drained of blood.

'This man. He—'

The tall, pale man had a gun in his hand. He raised it and fired. The man was thrown back against his car, blood on his crisp white shirt. He scrabbled at the smooth, rounded metal. He was choking, spittle and blood at his mouth. And then he was lying on the road, hunched up. The tall man walked over to him, quite slowly, and fired twice more.

After the sound of the shots, loud even in the open, Clemency's ears were ringing and the road seemed unnaturally quiet. The only sound was the water in the gulley and the gasping sobs from the man's wife. Unwilling, Clemency looked over to her. She had stumbled out of the car, and was gazing at them, one hand clenched in front of her mouth. There were no tears yet, her eyeliner and powder unmarked. Her pale green mohair suit, the matching round hat, the beautifully styled hair, were all immaculate, and made a shocking contrast to the sickly face, the slack mouth and the frightened eyes.

She looked round at them all, even at Clemency, as if they were all guilty. And she turned and ran.

Her movements were awkward, as if she had never tried to run before, her heels kicking out, her arms lifted up. And the Russian's long stride meant he was almost as fast, while still walking. He could no doubt have caught her in a few steps. Instead, he raised the gun and fired. Her back arched, her arms flung out, her knees buckled and she crumpled to the ground. Again, unhurried, he walked over to her and fired twice more.

'Take his wallet,' he called over to the driver. 'Her jewels and handbag. Check their luggage for valuables. Then put them in the car and roll it into the ravine.'

A hold-up gone wrong: so obvious, but so neat. And still Petrov's mind was in command of the situation. Under his directions, one of them heaved the dead man up under his shoulders and began to drag him towards the car. The other man had the dead woman by the arms, pulling her along. One of her shoes came off and he grunted with annoyance.

'What about the girl?'

Petrov thought.

There had been a game at Clemency's school, a version of truth or dare: what would you do if the four-minute warning sounded? Which teacher you would kiss, or how much gin you could drink in the time allowed before atomic incineraton? How many rules you could break? What was the truth you always wanted to tell your worst enemy or your closest friend?

A few moments were all she had left. There would be no partying in the face of death; no last stolen kiss; no declaration of love beyond the shadows. Just fear, kneeling on the roadway; pain; and then it would be her body being dragged to one of the cars; her lifeblood staining the grey tarmac.

Petrov walked towards her, so, so, slowly. He was checking his pistol. He would shoot her, and she would fall to the ground. Then he would shoot her twice more. It was what they did. She could see that. Routine.

He stood over her, his face in shadow against the beautiful blue sky.

Did he want her to plead for her life? No. He was a professional. There was nothing personal in this. No pleasure. Just a job to be done.

He crouched down and touched the end of her nose lightly with the tip of the gun.

'You tell the police it was a robbery. Bandits. They had masks. You know nothing. Tell them that. Then, he will live.'

He nodded at Peter, standing slumped against the bonnet of the Mercedes.

'If you say one word about us to the police, then he will die. I will see to it personally. Yes? And one other thing you must do for me.'

He stopped and slowly, lovingly, he let the barrel of the gun touch her lips, and then down the line of her throat, until it lay between her breasts.

'Go back to your office, little girl. Tell them this is

not a game. It is not for amateurs and fools and stupid children.'

The gun moved lower. There was nothing cold or calculating in his eyes. This wasn't just a job any more. The only reason she was to live was because he was taking more pleasure in humiliating her than he would take in killing her. He would have this moment to savour later, in private; or perhaps in bed with his wife or his mistress.

'Can you hear me, little girl?'

She licked her lips. The taste of the metal was sour, sickening.

She couldn't speak; but she nodded; and that was the worst of all.

Then he was gone, a spring in his step, back to his men, arranging the last move in the game. Peter's hands were already bound behind his back. Now they hustled him over to the Mercedes. Just before they forced down his head and pushed him into the back seat, he looked over to where Clemency lay sprawled on the road and his expression of helplessness was worse than anything.

The engine started, and after a last look around, satisfied with his work, Petrov climbed into the front passenger seat. The car drove off, and Clemency had a last glimpse of Peter's white face staring through the rear window.

21

Swan was furious. Operation ROSEWATER was a bust, and there was no one with whom to share the blame. He'd had to drop everything, even a meeting with the Minister, to borrow a RAF Dominie and fly out to Annecy. He hated France, mountains and rain in equal measure, and as he was driven north into the Jura, he was surrounded by all three. But there were too many loose ends for him to try and wrap things up from London.

Starting with the girl. What did she know? Would she cause trouble? He'd be meeting her in half an hour; which was why he'd asked Roberts to meet him at the airfield.

'How's she taking it?'

'Remarkably well,' Roberts replied. 'She got herself off the mountain before the police arrived. She took her suitcase, too, so there's no reason for them to suspect there was anyone else with Major Aspinal when he crashed.'

'That's something, I suppose.'

'She even left a note on the windscreen saying *Police Aware*. That's why no-one called the *gendarmes* until this morning. I thought that was pretty smart thinking, after what she'd been through.'

'It sounds as if you're as susceptible to Miss White's charms as Aspinal was,' Swan said sourly. 'Where is she now?'

'At the hotel. Seaton and I have been taking her through what happened. He's gone to check the chalet they were staying in for any loose ends and his wife is keeping her company. We also got a tame doctor out. There's nothing physically wrong with her – a few cuts and bruises – but we've explained to the hotel that she's not very well.'

'Under her own name?'

'Yes. That was the only passport she had.'

Swan stared out of the car window, where the rain was turning to sleet as they climbed out of the valley. The hiss of the slush under the tyres merged with the mindless beat of the windscreen wipers.

None of this was going to sound good in his report. But really, it was impossible trying to put these operations together with the slim resources at his disposal. To do it properly would have needed another two men to ride shotgun, two more to make sure Aspinal's tail was clear, and a pro in place of the girl. Instead, it had been another mission with too much risk built in. This time, as was bound to happen in the end, they hadn't got away with it.

'What's your status with the local police?'

'I'm here as one of the consular staff. They're assuming it's a motor accident. The only problem is when they find the other bodies.'

'The what?' Swan had listened to the recording of the girl's call on the emergency number, and there'd been no mention of more deaths.

'A couple of civilians turned up at the wrong moment and got caught up in it. The other side killed them. Then they put them in their car and ran it off the road and into a ravine. The problem is, the police theory is that Aspinal might have concussion and be wandering about somewhere nearby. They're mounting a search and so they're bound to find the other car.'

'Christ Almighty. Who were they?'

'A French couple. Well-off. Someone will miss them

before the day is out, even if the police weren't searching the area.'

'Well, maybe in all this…' Swan said, looking out at the fading light, the teeming rain. 'No chance of getting a helicopter up.'

Roberts stayed silent.

'Will she keep her mouth shut?' Swan asked. 'The last thing we need is a hysterical girl talking to the press. Particularly the French ones.'

'Her main concern is that we get Aspinal back.'

'I take it they got the tape? I don't know why Peter didn't just stick the bloody thing in the post at the nearest town. Or scrub the whole pick-up. He knew the opposition were around, didn't he?'

'Not quite. The girl thought she saw Petrov in the village, but Aspinal wasn't convinced. She thinks he thought she was imagining it. You know, if you're keyed up and start seeing ghosts.'

'Petrov,' Swan said, half to himself. 'That's the last bloody straw. Our Russian friends have some choice bastards working for them, Roberts, but Petrov is the worst of the lot.'

◊

They had been kind to her. Kind, but ruthless in extracting every detail. Because it could still, perhaps, save Peter, she had made herself go through it all again and again. Descriptions of the four men. Every word Petrov had said. Even a description of the pistol he had held. The only thing she held back was the way he had touched her with it.

And each hour, each minute, it became more and more unbearable. Peter being taken away from her made her panic, left her with voices screaming inside her, telling her to find him, save him. She sat so still, so calm, because any move might make her shatter like glass.

When Swan arrived, bringing authority and power into the small bedroom, she felt reassured. Still in his coat, he sat in the single armchair, and she sat on the bed, and the other two men stood in attendance on him, and he asked a few questions and at once seemed to understand the whole situation.

'Right, Miss White, I'm sorry to have to ask you to go through this all again, but there's a good chance he's still in France. I don't think their intention was to kidnap him. That is probably a by-product of how things have played out. If so, it will take them a few days to sort something out. That gives us an opening. I've had a very informal conversation with my opposite number in the French intelligence service and I'm hopeful they may have a lead.'

Despite her tiredness, she concentrated on telling her story as best she could, for Swan was the one who could mobilise the power of the French state, so they were no longer a small group in a cheap provincial hotel, but connected to hundreds of thousands of police, gendarmes, agents, in every corner of France.

'And after they'd gone?' he asked.

'I took my bags and walked down the road for a couple of miles. There wasn't any other traffic. I suppose those poor people were just so unlucky to come along at that exact moment.'

She stopped and bit her lip.

'No need to dwell on that,' Sawn said, and it was so like her father's 'doctor's voice', the easy assurance that all would be well that was calming and annoying in equal measure. 'Tell me how you got to the hotel.'

'There was a little village. In the end a bus came. It came here. That was the end of the line. I found this place. And called you.'

Her thoughts were becoming less fluent as tiredness caught up on her. If this had been an interrogation, it would have been the signal to up the pressure, to force her to go over the story again and again to flush out the discrepancies that would lead to the lies and then, in the end, to the truth.

But Swan believed her, as much as he believed anyone about anything. Somehow, she had avoided falling into the hands of the French police, nor left any trace in Peter's car. A professional could not have done much better. He'd once commented to a colleague that Peter Aspinal would be a better officer if he spent less time thinking with his prick. On this occasion at least, he had chosen wisely. But it also meant that he'd have to handle the girl with some circumspection. If she wished it, she could make a lot of trouble.

◊

Swan didn't spend a lot of time confiding in his subordinates; but it was helpful in having Roberts as a sounding-board as he reflected on what could be saved from the sinking ship that was ROSEWATER, or indeed how it could be scuttled with the minimum of fuss. The rain had moved on, and they walked a little way until there were fields on either side and no-one to overhear them except some sodden and incurious cows.

'Quite a story,' he said. 'Do you think she's told us everything she knows?'

'They usually hold something back, don't they?'

Roberts replied. 'It's whether it's important or not. But she admitted killing the GRU man, Temnikov.'

'Yes, that was odd, wasn't it? If I'd heard that you'd burst in on a couple of Moscow hoods, held them up at gunpoint, shot one of them dead, rescued a hostage and then escaped on ski with a secret tape, I'd have put you in for an OBE. She didn't describe it like that, of course, but that's what it amounts to. And she's a cypher clerk with no training.'

'She told me that she'd been given some instruction by an old colleague of Aspinal's in Bern. A former SOE operative.'

'Really? SOE always were ones to shoot first and not bother to ask questions later. And now she just sits quietly telling us she shot someone through the eye, because all she cares about is getting her man back.'

'Is there any chance?'

'The more we say we want him back, the more they'll think he knows something. Then, whatever we offer, they'll try and get him over to Moscow and give him the full treatment. If he survives that, then they may trade him. But if we press too hard now – particularly if we bring the French in – then they may decide he's too hot to try and smuggle out. Then it really will be a bullet in the back of the head.'

'You can't tell her that.'

'God, no. She might seem quite level-headed, but there's every chance she'd go off at the deep end. The last thing what's left of this operation needs is a hysterical female running around writing to her MP about betrayal in the secret service. No, we'll have to play it long.'

He stopped and checked his watch.

'My man in the *Deuxième* says there's a group of Soviet trade officials over meeting pharmaceutical firms in Provence. Two men and a woman in their twenties, and an older man.' He glanced at a scrap of paper. 'One metre seventy-two, about eighty kilos, thinning dark brown hair, brown eyes, dark complexion, small scar on chin. That one could be Petrov. They're staying at a hotel in Nice.

'They're sure it's him?'

'No, and they aren't following up on it yet either. I've used up a lot of favours on this. We'll identify him and then discuss what to do with him with the French.'

'And the tape?' Roberts asked.

'He'll have that with him, I'm sure. Or rather, hidden nearby. He won't want to be picked up with it on him, but he won't want it far out of his sight either.'

'Shall I ask London to have a photo of Petrov sent out.'

'Oh, we can do better than that. We have someone who knows him rather intimately, don't we?'

22

They set off within the hour. Roberts was driving, Swan silent at his side, except for occasionally giving directions, and Clemency curled up on the back seat, under a pile of coats. She dozed from time to time, for the noise of the engine, the darkness outside, the sense of movement and purpose, were all soothing. And when she was awake, there was the sight of Swan, heavy and implacable, lit by the instrument panel. She had been driven like this many times before, years ago, with her father at the wheel and her mother with the maps, and there had been the same sense of absolute security. They would find Petrov, and Swan would find a way of getting Peter back.

The journey took all night, their route winding up into the mountains once more, with diversions where the passes were closed with snow. But the two men seemed to know where they were, with occasional terse exchanges about the RN202, the Col de la Cayolle and the advantages of a detour via Serres or Digne.

They stopped only twice. Once was for petrol, the other at a shack by the side of the road to buy coffee and a scratch meal of dry sausage and stale baguette. For this she got out of the car and stood by the roadside, watching the sparse traffic – mainly trucks at this time of night, taking advantage of the clear roads – and taking in the smell of the icy air and the pines. She accepted a dash of whisky in her coffee, and it helped wash down the food, and now the two men were her colleagues, and could she ask them about their plans for when they reached Nice, and what her role would be. But Swan, it seemed, had no particular plan. It all depended on the layout of the hotel.

She dozed again, waking as the dawn approached and they were coming out of the mountains in the grey light, more people on the roads now, cafés taking down their shutters, and from one hairpin bend, a glimpse of the blue of the Mediterranean.

The Hotel Worcester was on the edge of the old town, one street back from the promenade, and built in the massive style of the Edwardian years, taking up almost a whole block with its faded stone and ornate ironwork. They were able to park a little way down the narrow street, and this commanded a fine view of the steps of the main entrance; except that there was another exit to the rear, and a third way out through the restaurant.

'Why don't we wait in the lobby?' Clemency suggested. 'He doesn't know you, and I could wear a veil.'

Swan had an aversion to disguises. They were amateur, unreliable, even ridiculous; but he could see no alternative. He went in and booked a room while Clemency wrote out exact instructions and measurements for Roberts to take to the nearest shop that would sell him a ready-made black suit, gloves, hat and veil. The only risk was the few moments between the door and the lift; but with a handkerchief to her face, they completed this successfully. She changed quickly, reassured herself and Swan that no one could make out her features under the thick veil, and they walked back down to the lift.

'Remember, all we want you to do is to sit and watch when he comes past. If it's him, don't say anything, don't react at all. He can't see your face, and if you don't stand up – particularly if he doesn't see you walking – he's very unlikely to make the connection.'

'What if he does?'

'Don't worry. We'll be there.'

The bell rang to announce the lift was arriving.

'Are you sure you can pull this off?' Swan said quietly. 'I mean, playing the part of a widow.'

She thought of Peter; of Swan's ill-concealed pessimism; her fear that Peter was already dead.

'Don't worry, Mr Swan. I won't need to put on an act.'

◊

They had warned her that a stakeout was the most boring, most frustrating experience imaginable. Only those with extraordinary patience – the kind of mind that liked to spend a day on a riverbank fishing or reassembling a jigsaw of a thousand pieces – could find any enjoyment in it. Roberts and Swan both became unsettled as the morning wore on, rereading their papers, shifting in their seats, thinking up excuses to get up and move around. But Clemency sat with her back straight, gazing across the lobby to the brass and dark oak of the reception desk, watching the trickle of guests coming and going, studying the way they walked, their voice as they asked for their keys or if there were any messages; their faces as they glanced to their left across the tables and chairs of the piano bar, and paid no attention to the young widow and the two men – *an uncle, perhaps? A brother? No, the older one was surely the lawyer* – sitting by the window.

The ache in her back from sleeping in the car; the tiredness that kept trying to envelop her, so that she had to pinch the inside of her arm above her elbow to stay awake; these she was glad to suffer. Peter would have done the same – a hundred times more – for her.

Swan made a couple of long-distance calls – she could see him in the phone boxes by the passage through to the toilets. But whatever he learned, he shared none of it with her or with Roberts. He also spent some time chatting to one of the staff at the reception desk, and she guessed that he had bribed the clerk for some information about Petrov.

Lunch came and went; sandwiches and a half-bottle of wine for the two men, and nothing but coffee for Clemency, even though they said she should eat to keep up her strength. After that distraction, they settled back into watchful boredom.

Then a party of three men and a woman came through the main entrance and up to the desk. They were dressed in business suits, the men carrying attaché cases and the woman what looked like a portable typewriter in a case with a shoulder-strap. They were laughing about something and had the relaxed air of having finished their work for the day.

Petrov was the leader, the one the others deferred to; it was so clearly him that she forgot to give some sign to the others. Instead she continued to stare, because it was beyond belief that the man could be so evil and yet be so much at home in the world of agreeable hotels, the sunshine and the sea only a street away, the group of colleagues chatting so pleasantly.

They picked up their keys and moved to wait for the lift. Petrov was the oldest, the two other men were in their twenties, perhaps with more muscle and shorter hair than would be usual in the business world. They were speaking in Russian, and she wondered how they could be so blatant, and why the French intelligence service were letting them wander about unsupervised; unless perhaps one of the other guests sitting about in the bar were keeping them under discreet surveillance.

The lift came, and they were gone, and Clemency let out her breath. Swan leaned forward.

'Him?'

'Yes.'

'How sure are you?'

She thought of how Petrov had crouched beside her, rested the gun against her, looked into her eyes and smiled. She would know him in the depths of hell.

'Completely sure.'

'Good. The question is, what do we do about it.'

The way Swan said it, he clearly did not want opinions from the others, but was marshalling his own thoughts. But Clemency could not help but speak.

'Won't the French arrest him?'

'Only if there's some evidence. He and his colleagues are here legally as part of a trade mission. We know where they were over the weekend, but without proof, we can't get the French to move against them. It would be the equivalent of breaking diplomatic immunity.'

'But I'm a witness.'

'They may say that, as you work for the British government, you are not impartial.'

'If they found the bodies of the French couple, that might wake them up,' Roberts offered. 'Perhaps an anonymous call…'

'I don't think we want to kick that ant's nest, John,' Swan said, with an edge to his voice, and Clemency realised that Swan wasn't thinking aloud, but was leading her along a path he had already mapped out, leading her so she would agree with the course of action – or inaction – that he had fixed upon; and he didn't want any helpful suggestions from his underling.

'As far as we know, they are here until tomorrow. That gives us time to open negotiations. The only problem is, what leverage do we have? They have Peter, and they have the tape. It's possible that…'

Swan carried on setting out his view of the situation, and Clemency became more and more sure that this was all intended to justify to her, maybe even to himself, that he did not plan to do anything at all about Peter. It could have been the Ambassador or Dansby-Gregg producing these jewel-like, meaningless phrases: *could do more harm than good… important not to blunder in until we know all the facts… repercussions of making a formal request to the French authorities…* And having set himself up to fail, he gave the impression of action.

'There's no reason to let him know we're on the spot. I'll telephone London from here and get them to patch a call through back to the hotel. Then I'll sound Petrov out in general terms and see what he might accept. John, why don't you take Miss White out for a walk? This could take a while.'

Despite the blue sky and the palm trees, it was hard to imagine how the town would be in the summer. The bars along the promenade were closed, the beach clubs shuttered, and the few visitors, walking their miniature dogs or sitting sour-faced over coffee and cake, were all elderly. It fitted Clemency's mood, and she told herself she was coming to terms with what she had always known, ever since Petrov's car had driven off, leaving her sobbing in the dust by the roadside.

She would never see Peter again.

But like a bonfire in the rain, there was beneath the sodden leaves of misery a smouldering core of anger. The more she thought of Swan and his unwillingness to take a risk, to tell the French everything, to make some waves while there was a chance of saving Peter, the more that anger flared and spread.

'I'm so glad that the French authorities are co-operating,' she said. 'I thought they'd be furious about us operating in France without their permission.'

'Yes,' Roberts replied, relieved for the break in the oppressive silence. 'Of course, the contacts at the moment are entirely informal.'

'It's usually best to keep it that way, isn't it?'

'Yes, absolutely. The Old Boys net, and all that. Once you make a formal request, a lot more people have to know at both ends. Much better to sort things out quietly.'

'And if we'd involved the French from the start, they'd have expected us to share what we got.'

'Quite. Which wouldn't have been fair. I mean, Peter had done all the work. Made the contact, taken the risks. Well, Peter and you, of course.'

They walked on. As she had suspected, neither Peter nor London had told the French about the operation. Now it had all gone wrong, including two dead French citizens, Swan didn't want to admit to this formally. Probably his French counterparts wouldn't want that either. A roadside robbery was one thing; a clash between two foreign secret services on French soil would make the French intelligence people look rather stupid.

They lingered over coffee, with Clemency becoming

more withdrawn, and Roberts's conversational gambits falling more and more flat. She was happy to let the cold seep into her bones, leaving her numb. She wanted to stay there forever, if it meant postponing her return to the hotel, and hearing the news from Swan. In the end, Roberts had to insist.

As soon as she was back in the hotel room, Swan sat her down and poured her a drink. Then, a little ill at ease, he explained that Petrov would not do a deal.

'I'm sorry, Miss White. But don't give up. Once he's in the Soviet Union, we can start to try and set up an exchange. It's been done many times before, you know.'

'How is he?'

'Well, naturally Petrov didn't say anything about that. We were talking in code, you know. I asked about a swop, and he said he did not think the time was ripe, or words to that effect.'

Although she had thought that Swan would let Peter down, the totality of his betrayal still surprised her. He was, it seemed, preparing to leave at once. Roberts, too, was to go back to Grenoble to liaise with the local police.

'You're very welcome to come with us,' Swan said without any enthusiasm. 'But you may be more comfortable going by train. Or you could stay on here for a few days. The office will pick up the tab. Give you a chance to... well... get over things before you go back to Bern.'

She didn't want to be there on her own, but the idea of leaving Petrov was worse. Swan, uneasy that he could not read her mood, suggested that they should all go and have something to eat and then decide. They left her few possessions in the room and took the lift.

It stopped on the floor below to let in two more guests: Petrov and his secretary.

Clemency backed away instinctively and ended up standing almost behind Petrov, convinced he would recognise her. Roberts was looking studiously away, as if worried she might try and confront Petrov. And perhaps, if Peter's gun had been in her handbag, she might have shot him there and then.

The lift stopped on the seventh, this time for a woman well into her seventies, her sharp nose pointing out from a wrap of dead fox. They shuffled round to make room and the bag that Petrov's secretary had slung over her shoulder bumped against Clemency.

'*Pardonnez-moi,*' the girl said, and then, perhaps to recognise Clemency's status as a grieving widow, added a little smile of sympathy and apology. Clemency nodded in response, in case even a single word might reveal her identity to Petrov.

From behind the flimsy protection of her veil, she studied the girl: about her own age, maybe an inch shorter, and very Russian, fair with high cheekbones. She looked the part of a secretary, with her plain dark suit and the portable typewriter, but she must be a GRU officer. She suspected the Soviets didn't use amateurs for their espionage.

Then Petrov half-turned and spoke to the girl in Russian. Clemency got the gist of it – that they had earned the best dinner in the flower market – but it was the girl's reaction that revealed their relationship. She was more of a Soviet reflection of Clemency than was comfortable, down to her feelings for her boss. Tonight, instead of Peter and Clemency, it would be Petrov and the girl who would be dining together, celebrating the success of their mission.

If she'd had the gun, she might have killed them both.

The doors opened on the ground floor and they all shuffled out, Clemency watching the two Russians as they placed their keys on the reception desk and headed out for *aperitifs*. The girl's room was 727; directly below Clemency's. She was glad she would soon be gone; to listen to Petrov and Russian girl enjoying each other that night, after returning from dinner, would be intolerable. And yet...

'Well done, Miss White,' Swan said. 'You played that very well.'

She didn't reply. She was far too absorbed in working out how she, and she alone, could free Peter. Only when Swan spoke again did she respond.

'I don't think I can eat anything,' she said. 'I'm going to go back up to my room and try to sleep. I'll come back to Bern tomorrow.'

'That's a good idea,' Swan said, evidently relieved to be shot of her. 'Roberts, I think we might set out straight away and have something on the road. We'll be in touch once you're back in Bern tomorrow. Obviously not a word of any of this to anyone, including the Ambassador. The more we can keep this to ourselves, the more chance of getting Peter back.'

His self-interest was so blatant that it made her feel sick. But she agreed with everything he said, simply to get rid of them both so she could begin to think, to plan.

'Do you have everything you need?' he said. 'Money and so on?'

'Yes, thank you.' That at least was true. Peter had made sure she had a wad of travellers' cheques, together with her passport, her Swiss diplomatic identity card and her driver's licence. He said that having money and papers gave you manoeuvrability, options. At the time, it had seemed pointless; playing at being spies. Now it might just save his life.

She watched them go, then went over to the reception desk.

'Could you make up my bill, please? I'll need to leave very early in the morning. And send up coffee and some sandwiches to my room? And I shall need to hire a car.'

23

As she prepared herself, it was a comfort that with every step, every link in the plan, Peter was with her.

First, she left the hotel and, from the opposite pavement, spent ten minutes studying its ornate frontage, including the spotlights and the pools of shadow they left; and thought of Peter's words on the need for reconnaissance.

Then she returned to her room and took the gun from the bottom of her suitcase. She stripped it, just as he had shown her, cleaned and oiled it, and reassembled it. Then she laid it ready on the bed.

She drew the curtains and switched off the lights, and then practiced moving silently around the darkened room, memorising the position of the bed, table and chair, the window and the light switches, and the doors to the bathroom and the corridor.

Then it was time to wait; hours punctuated first by the return of her passport and driving licence, along with the key to a nearly-new Renault Dauphine, now parked in a side street; then by the coffee and sandwiches.

At last it was time. Amongst other tricks of the trade, Lucinda had shown her how to pick a lock; but for that, she'd had a set of skeleton keys, and without those, there was no chance of Clemency opening a hotel door fitted with Ingersolls. But she'd also learned how to flip up the latch of a window using only a strip of celluloid, and she had practised this on her own French windows that gave onto the tiny balcony. So that was the way she would have to go.

Climbing up the lift shaft at the party, months ago it seemed now, she had struggled, constrained by the maid's costume. Now she wore her black leotard, black gloves, and a dark silk scarf worn as a mask. Free to move, and to move without being seen, she stepped onto the tiny balcony and looked down. No-one would be watching; she was at one with the night. She climbed over the ironwork of the balcony, swung round, and reached out with her foot for the ledge. It was only just in reach, leaving her stretched over the void, the fall of eight stories to the asphalt below. But she felt no fear. It was duty that drove her on, fatalism that kept her sedated.

After that, reaching the floor below was easy. The late-Empire frontage had an abundance of cornices, corbels and embrasures, down which she could climb until she was ready to drop onto the balcony of the room below; room 727.

The drop, the passing traffic, the thought of what the fall would do to her; it all meant nothing. She simply kept herself poised, on the balls of her feet, her muscles taut, but not overstretched, just like those long-ago lessons in the gymnasium.

She landed lightly, went into a crouch instinctively; checked her gun was still in the belt at her waist.

In a moment, she had the windows open and was in the room, looking around, talking her time, absorbing that atmosphere. As Peter had said, a mission was to be taken at pace, but never rushed.

She searched the room carefully, in case her guess about the location of the missing tape was wrong. She found a few traces of this other girl: a copy of *Paris-Match*, perhaps providing her with glimpses of a world more alluring that that of Moscow; a packet of mints in the bedside cabinet; some surprisingly glamorous nightwear laid out by the pillow. But no tape.

The plan of the room was identical to her own, and Clemency had worked out where she wanted to be when the Russian girl returned: sitting on the floor by the bed, so that she could choose her moment to reveal her presence. She'd have at least an hour to wait. Petrov was there in the character of a fun-loving trade official, on a spree away from the constraints of Moscow, and of course he would be visiting bars, nightclubs, enjoying every minute. It would be the right cover, and why shouldn't he celebrate? He had pulled off a coup, putting Peter and the tape into the bag.

She glanced at her wrist-watch. A quarter to midnight.

She felt oddly close to Peter, sitting with her back against the cold plaster. She imagined him waiting in her room for her to return and report, then listening to her breathless, excited account of her adventures with that mix of amusement and respect that she found irresistible.

She made herself relax her grip on the butt of the gun; eased her tensed fingers; stretched out her legs to dispel the beginnings of cramp.

Then there were footsteps in the corridor, voices, much sooner than she had expected. Russian voices: the man's, low and confident; the woman's, lighter, clearer. They paused outside the door.

Flirting; not wanting the evening to end.

But before Clemency could begin to think what she would do if Petrov came in, they parted. The key in the lock. The door opening.

The girl humming a tune to herself.

Clemency had risen to rest on her haunches, gun

in one hand, the other touching the wall for balance. For a moment, she was back in the clerks' room in the Embassy in Bern; at school; at home; a long line of Clemencys leading up to this moment. It was as if she were watching herself in a play, performing a role that could never be truly her.

The light flicked on. She had her eyes half-closed, expecting it.

The girl crossed the room, put her bag on the table and then took off her coat, her scarf, then sitting to remove her boots. That done, she stood and began to unbutton her jacket.

'Comrade.'

Clemency's voice croaked a little. The Russian girl swung round, saw the gun, froze, one hand to her open mouth, her eyes wide.

Clemency put her finger to her lips; after a moment, the girl nodded. Then she pointed to the floor, and clumsily, fearfully, the girl lay down. Clemency had taken the cord from the curtains in her own room and tied them into loops with slip knots, ready to bind the girl's wrists and ankles. But as she approached, the door behind her opened.

'Larissa?'

Petrov was standing in the connecting doorway to his own room, wearing nothing but a towelling robe. Instead of his colleague lying pouting on the bed, waiting for him in flimsy underwear, he was presented with a sinister figure in black, holding a silenced pistol. But if he were alarmed, he didn't show it.

'Who are you?' he demanded. 'What do you want?'

Tempo, Peter had called it, when he beat her at chess, and when he told her his philosophy of covert operations. Never give the opposition time to get back onto the front foot. Maintain the initiative. Develop your plans so quickly that they cannot respond.

She fired a shot into the thin-legged writing desk. Pieces of cheap wood flew across the room, followed by the sweet smell of gunpowder. The noise would not even have carried to the next room.

Before he could react, the gun was pointing at his heart.

'Kneel.'

Grudgingly he did so, complaining about his status as a diplomat, his desire to contact the Soviet consul, the risk of an international incident.

She removed her mask, and there was enough light from the street outside for him to recognise her. But there was not the shock, the fear, she had counted on. If anything, he seemed amused.

'And what can I do for you, little girl?'

'I've come for the tape.'

'I don't know what you mean.'

He said it with a sneer; not to try and convince her he was innocent, but to show he didn't care, that she was no threat to him, that this was a boring interlude until he either went away empty-handed or he decided to escape and deal with her himself.

'I know nothing. Why don't you take my watch, little girl, or my wallet? Like a tart that does not make enough from her tricks, eh?'

She stood behind him; rested the gun against his neck and leaned over to whisper in his ear.

'I want nothing more in the world than to kill you. But I have my orders. If you do as I say, I have to let you live.'

She gestured to the Russian girl, Larissa, to come over and use the cords to tie Petrov to the frame of the bed. She was reluctant – just as scared of him as she was of the gun – but in the end he told her impatiently to get it done. Clemency watched as she pulled them tight. Then she climbed onto the bed herself to check he was secured.

Still watching them both warily, she went to the table where the typewriter lay. Except that wasn't what it was. Standing at the girl's side, in the lift, Clemency had seen the single word on the lid: GRUNDIG. They didn't make typewriters; they made tape recorders. A simple way to hide something secret in plain sight; and for her to have every reason, as a good secretary, to carry it with her everywhere.

Clemency flipped the lock and opened the lid. There inside, built so neatly into the space, was a reel-to-reel tape recorder. She examined it for a moment – she'd used machines like this before, but not this make – and then turned one of the switches. The tape began to run through the spindles and across the magnetic heads. She turned up the volume and there was a curious sound, a high-speed electronic clatter, without pattern or meaning, just a stream of information that spoke of underground bunkers lined with electrical equipment, men in white coats making notes on clipboards.

She rewound the tape until the end was freed and slapping round and round. Then she released the spool from the spindle and turned to Petrov.

But her discovery of the tape did not seem to worry him. He was cool, almost amused.

'Why do you want the tape?' he asked. 'Not for your department. They would never have agreed to this nonsense. Not for yourself. What use could it be for you? Except if you think it is worth something in exchange. Yes. Of course. For Major Aspinal. You find the tape, and then you tell me I can have it back if I let him go. Is that it? Little girl, you are playing a game, and yet I do not think you know the rules.'

'It's simple enough: the tape for Peter.'

He just laughed.

'Of course not. But I am pleased to see you are ready to betray your country for some sex. Was he the best, eh? Do you miss him already in the long winter nights? I had not thought the English were so passionate.'

It was all wrong. He was the one tied to the frame of the bed; she was the one with the gun in her hand. Yet he was in command, mocking her.

'What now, little girl? I think you had better run away.'

'We can trade,' she said desperately. 'There are Soviet spies in prison in England.'

'No.'

He spoke so assuredly, his last word on the subject. She had no idea what to do.

As if he knew he had the advantage, that she was on the point of freezing, he leaned back on the bed.

'Even if I wished to make this exchange, what is your plan? How would we trade? Such things need finesse, preparation, some way to ensure that both sides do as they promise. And then—'

Clemency remembered Larissa just as the blow landed on her neck. She rolled off the bed and lay on the floor, gasping for breath. There was an arm round her neck, a judo hold, legs locked around Clemency's ankles. She twisted desperately, fought her way to her feet, Larissa still on her back.

Clemency stumbled backwards and rammed into the wall. The girl cried out as the light switch cut into her back. And now Clemency was free of her, dropping to her knees, gasping for air, massaging her bruised neck.

The gun was gone, out of sight.

She waited too long. Larissa was back. She had the scarf in her hands. Now it was round Clemency's neck, pulled tight. Petrov was shouting, encouraging her with venom: *harder, pull it harder, you bitch, twist it!* Clemency couldn't get her finger-nails under the fabric. Trying was wasting time. She had so little time left.

As Lucinda had shown her, she dropped her shoulder and twisted round. The girl came with her, they fell to the floor, Clemency on top, and the other girl winded.

Now she had her knee in Larissa's back, the scarf round her neck. Time seemed to stand still, with Larissa twisting, arching her back to try and throw Clemency off. She clawed at the carpet, choking, spittle at her lips, her eyes flashing with rage and terror.

Then, suddenly, it was over, the girl lying limp beneath her.

In the end, it was a furtive, scraping sound that brought Clemency back to reality; a sound that could have been a rat in the wainscot, but was actually Petrov trying to pull the cords apart with his teeth.

Still he showed no fear.

'What now?' he asked, as if merely curious. 'This will not look very good to the French police.'

Clemency found there were tears in her eyes. She looked down on the girl lying so still, then climbed hurriedly to her feet.

'Is that all you care?'

'Why should I care? She was nothing. She was to pass the time for tonight. She should have killed you when she had the chance. You, on the other hand, you have the instinct of a killer.'

Why was he taunting her? Was it to rile her into making a mistake?

'But you were coming to her bed,' she protested.

'More fool her. Maybe she thought it would help her career.'

'*Ублюдок!*'

Larissa was pushing herself upright, grimacing, one hand to her throat. Petrov spat something back at her. Then they were trading insults in a raid flow of colloquial Russian that Clemency had no hope of following. She stepped over her, grabbed her wrists and quickly bound them together with her scarf. The Russian girl was in no state to resist, and hardly seemed to care, so great was her disgust with Petrov.

They kept trading insults as Clemency went to the wardrobe, pulled out a blouse and she tore at the arms until they came free. She used one as a gag on Petrov; none too soon, as he had said something that had turned Larissa as white as a sheet. She was shaking as Clemency lifted her to her feet, guided her into the bathroom and tied her to one of the water pipes.

The girl was begging in a low, desperate voice, too quickly for Clemency to follow. In any case, time was running short. She twisted the sleeve into another gag and tied it round her mouth. The girl kept trying to speak, squirming in frustration, her eyes pleading, as if Clemency was about to kill her in cold blood.

Was that because it was the right thing to do?

Larissa was the perfect cover for Petrov's liquidation. Presented with a mistress shot through the heart, and a lover who had put a bullet through his own brain in remorse, the French police would stamp it *crime passionnel* and close the file. French intelligence might suspect there was more to it than that, but by then Clemency would be safely back in Switzerland.

And the alternative? As soon as she left the room, they would both start signalling for help, kicking the walls and tapping on the pipes.

If she killed Petrov, it was the end of any hope of saving Peter. But Petrov would not co-operate. He thought she was bluffing. And the only way to prove she wasn't would be to kill him.

Or the girl.

She stood in the bathroom doorway, looking first at Petrov, who stared back at her insolently from the bed, like a chess grandmaster waiting for his opponent to make the next move; and Larissa, kneeling by the side of the bath, silent, awaiting her execution.

She looked at the gun in her hand. Peter had said it was a war. But that was not how she wanted to fight it.

She knelt down next to Larissa. It was ridiculous. A few minutes ago, each had tried to kill the other. Now Clemency was smiling in reassurance and producing some halting phrases of Russian to say she meant her no harm.

Despite this, the girl was shaking her head, imploring to be heard. Intrigued, Clemency eased the gag away from her mouth. She began to gabble in Russian. Then, with an effort, she switched to French.

'Don't leave me here. Petrov will have me killed.'

'He's just saying that.'

'No, it's true! He will not want a witness to this fiasco. If I am dead, he can blame me. Please! I can go to the police. They will give me asylum.'

Clemency shook her head, tightened the gag once more. She might believe her, but the thing was impossible. The Russian girl's training, her duty, would ensure that she freed Petrov, informed her superiors, joined the pursuit of Clemency and the tape. Sparing a prisoner was one thing; that was what soldiers did in wartime. But trusting her was another.

She gathered up their passports and other papers and their money – quite a lot of that – and then prepared to leave. She felt too battered to think of climbing back up to the room above, but she found a suit of Larissa's that would fit her well enough.

All the time she was conscious of Petrov's gaze; contemptuous of her, and triumphant because he had sensed her weakness, traded on it, and defeated her. Yes, she had the tape; but she had failed in her mission. Yes, he had lost the tape, but already he would be thinking that he would escape from his bonds before Larissa, and he would kill her, and say it was the British, and so the blame for the loss would fall on her, not him.

She let herself out of the door and went back to her room to collect her luggage. Her bill was paid, and the Renault was where they had told her it would be. She let herself in, dropped her case and coat on the back seat. It started first time and for a moment she listened in relief to the steady pulse of the engine. An hour's drive and she would be free of any pursuit, lost in the maze of roads in mountains to the north of Nice. Then she could eat, and sleep.

Then, with a sigh, she switched the engine off again.

At the end of the street there was a pay phone. She found a few *centimes* and held them ready to feed in; though as it happened she didn't need them, for the number she dialled was 900.

The voice at the other end was brusque.

'*Police municipal.*'

'I am calling from the Hotel Worcester,' Clemency said. 'There has been an incident. One of the guests is trying to kill a girl. To strangle her. Room 727. You'd better hurry.'

'Oui,' the man said, as if this was the kind of thing people reported all the time. 'And you? Who are you?'

But Clemency had hung up.

24

Lucinda wore a long black coat, and she kept it on as they waited for their coffee, as if she wanted to be gone, back to her office, her new life; away from the past.

'You don't think he's dead, then?'

Lucinda's eyes were cold, and there were red smudges on her cheeks. She was angry at Clemency, and who could blame her? Six, the Foreign Office, Swan, Petrov: all were far away, and Clemency was there in front of her.

'We were lovers once, you know,' Lucinda said abruptly. 'Did he tell you?'

Clemency shook her head.

'No, he wouldn't. In Paris, after the Liberation. We had three weeks together. I'm not saying he was the love of my life, or any tripe like that. Only that afterwards, no-one else seemed quite to match up.'

Clemency nodded.

'And what was it all for?' Lucinda asked. 'Can you tell me?'

'They don't know. They wouldn't tell me if they did, but I'm sure they don't.'

'You're talking in riddles.'

'They were approached by some high-up Romanians. Five of them. Peter went out to meet them and I went along as cover. They offered to send us a sample of what they could get hold of. We were jumped by the GRU. They got the tape and Peter. And they sent me back to London to rub their noses in it. That's why they didn't kill me.'

'Whyever would they do that?'

'One of theirs was killed.'

'Oh. That's bad.'

Clemency gazed into her coffee cup.

'And the Romanians?' Lucinda said. 'What happened to them?'

'One of them died in a car crash yesterday. It was in a telegram yesterday from Bucharest. I don't know about the others.'

'I expect they're dead too. How senior were they?'

'One was a General in the Air Force. I don't think I ever knew his name. There was a senior Party man called Ion Mishcon. He was the one who died. There was Professor Nechita and Dr Râs, but they didn't count for much. The leader was called Petrescu.'

For a moment, Clemency was back at the table, listening to the Professor's gentle, sad voice; watching the General spearing his food; aware of the scrutiny of the inscrutable Dr Râs. And then on the boat, watching Petrescu pull himself out of the sea, the water streaming from his brown skin, the energy seeming to crackle around him.

'One of them was a traitor?'

'Or a patriot,' Clemency suggested. 'I still don't really know if they were working for themselves or for Romania, or for some Communist ideal.'

But Lucinda appeared to have lost interest. She was gazing out of the window now, even though it was steamed up and it was almost impossible to see anything, beyond the occasional shadow of a passer-by on the pavement.

'Which of them was it?' she asked, without looking at Clemency. 'Which of them betrayed Peter?'

'I don't know. How can I know? I only met them

for a few hours. I suppose I knew that something was wrong but…'

'What did you think?'

Clemency was startled by the intensity of Lucinda's question.

'I suppose… that none of it was real. They weren't traitors, and they didn't want the money. We were being used for something. I just don't know what.'

'I expect you do.'

Clemency had once had a teacher like this. Miss Murphy. She would never tell you the answer. She would force you to think until you found it for yourself.

She looked back over the last three months, and the pieces now lying discarded by the side of the board. The couple in the car; Petrov's nephew; Mishcon. Peter. None of them mattered to those playing the game, but if they had been sacrificed, maybe it was to a purpose. In which case, was she wrong to assume that the plan had misfired? Maybe it had worked as intended…

'The Soviets got the tape,' she said slowly. 'Maybe that was supposed to happen. And Mishcon is dead. Maybe that was planned as well. But why?'

She closed her eyes. The words were hard to find, the thoughts painful to form. It was like giving birth to something twisted and deformed.

'Maybe there was… no, that can't be it. Could they have wanted the Russians to know about the tape? For one of them to tell the Russians? Yes. That's it. There were five of them, and one of them was working for the Russians. So they – it has to be Petrescu, I suppose – arranged it all so that there is a tape, an English spy, and whoever is the spy tells their bosses in Moscow. Petrescu has him followed and bugged and so he knows it. And then the traitor dies in a road accident.'

'Yes.'

'So it was Mishcon.'

'Yes.'

Clemency's face puckered up in confusion.

'All that to expose one traitor?'

But for the Romanians, it had been so simple. Paris had been a game to make the British all the more eager. Then they had sent one of their people to St Quentin to pass Clemency the tape. After that, the British and the Russians had chased around, killing each other.

'What was on the tape?' Lucinda was asking.

'I don't know. I haven't given it to anyone yet.'

'Really?' For the first time, there was a hint of amusement in the older woman's gaze. 'Why is that? Are you still hoping to swap it for Peter?'

'No, but... I suppose that if I give it back, then it's the end of it all for me. They'll cut me out of the whole thing, won't they?'

'Oh yes.'

'And any chance I still have of helping Peter will be gone.'

'That's right. No door closes quite as firmly as the door at Broadway, if they decide you're no longer part of the club.'

They fell silent. The waiter came and cleared the neighbouring table.

'What now?'

'I'm flying to London in an hour. I have an appointment with a man called Swan.'

'Peter told me all about him. He'll tell you whatever you want to hear and then make sure he never sees you again.'

'I expect you're right,' Clemency replied. 'But he may be disappointed.'

◊

The coach from the airport dropped her at Victoria, and from there it was one stop on the tube to St James' Park. All of it was familiar, and yet she passed through it in a kind of dream, as if the other passengers, the ticket inspectors, the newspaper seller at the station exit, were behind plate glass. As instructed, she went to the plain doorway on Broadway and pressed the bell. The guard on the door was expecting her and led her to a plain meeting on the third floor. Swan and Roberts were waiting for her.

'How was your trip back to Bern, Miss White?'

'It was fine. I'm afraid I had to hire a car and then leave it at Annecy station. It might be difficult to get the deposit back.'

'Well, never mind. I'm sure the Office can cover that, in the circumstances. At least you weren't caught up in the trouble at the hotel.'

'Oh yes?'

'It's rather amusing, actually. Petrov was robbed, would you believe. Held up at gunpoint. Just goes to show that even the GRU aren't a match for the French underworld.'

'What happened to him?'

'Apparently he shouted the place down demanding police protection. It was all the more embarrassing as it turns out he was in bed with the girl agent who was supposed to be his secretary. Not that the French care too much about that. Almost expect it. Anyway, it doesn't seem to have upset their plans. They've flown back to Moscow.'

'And Peter?'

Swan adjusted his expression to one of heartfelt concern.

'Nothing new. But do believe me, Miss White. we're doing absolutely everything we can.'

'Is there anyone of theirs we could exchange?'

Swan looked pained.

'It doesn't work quite like that, I'm afraid. Once a Soviet agent is in the hands of the British police and the courts, there's not really anything we can do. We have surprisingly limited powers, you understand. Our best hope is to work behind the scenes. I appreciate this will be frustrating, but you really must leave it to us.'

'He said to me it was a war. I think he knew the risks.'

'I'm sure he did,' Swan said, with something of the air of a parson at a funeral. 'He was a very brave man, Miss White. It will be hard to replace him.'

'Yes. That's why I'm here.'

'I don't exactly see what you mean,' he said cautiously.

'I want to work for you.'

'Well, we have plenty of cipher clerks and so on. But we could let you know if there's a vacancy, couldn't we, Roberts?'

She leaned forward and placed the reel of the tape onto his desk.

'Peter and I were asked to bring this to you.'

He picked it up, turned it over.

'You took it from Petrov?'

She nodded. Swan allowed himself a raised eyebrow.

'And how exactly—'

'I've written you a report,' she interrupted, taking an envelope from her bag. 'What I want in return is your agreement that I can transfer to your department. Not as a cipher clerk. I mean doing the same work as Peter. Until he comes home.'

'Well, that's out of the question.'

'That's unfortunate.'

Swan's eyes were not that different from Petrov's; cold, and wary, and without a shred of compassion. But Swan could not read her as well as Petrov had; and she believed she could bluff him.

'I want to work for you, Mr Swan. But if not, then I will tell the world that you've betrayed Peter.'

Swan sat back, as if he'd been expecting this.

'You'd be wasting your time,' said dismissively. 'The papers would never print a word you said.'

'I can try.'

'You seem to forget that you've signed the Official Secrets Act. If you breathe a word of anything to do with this department or your work with Peter, you'd be tried in secret, convicted and sent to prison.'

'Times have changed,' she said. 'The newspapers won't keep quiet just because you ask them to. Not after Profumo. And think of the story. A war hero captured by the Soviets. His girlfriend fighting to get him back. An Establishment cover-up. Do you think the papers would miss out on that? And what about Parliament? I looked up which MPs asked the most questions about Philby and the other Cambridge spies. You think they won't be interested in my story? Won't ask questions in the House? I'll start with George Wigg and then there's—'

'All right,' he snapped. 'You've made your point. But what makes you think that kind of noise would help Peter?'

'I don't know. But if I were working for you, Mr Swan, then I'd know that Peter would never be forgotten. I wouldn't have to tell anyone anything.'

Swan was more angry than he could remember. That this chit of a girl…

But she was right. The papers would have a field day. And what he agreed now, and what he actually did, could be very different.

'Very well.'

He ignored Roberts's startled reaction. He was the one calling the shots. *Reculer pour mieux sauter,* the French said. Withdraw, the better to attack.

'I take it this offer of yours is real? You could begin at once?'

'Yes.'

'Good.' Abruptly, he stood up. 'We have an operation underway that could benefit from just your combination of skills. I'll need you back here by six o'clock. With a suitcase packed and your passport.'

She was startled; and a little alarmed. Fine. Whether she backed out or whether she went through with her bizarre proposal no longer mattered. It was like a fork in chess; he had her whatever she did.

Roberts escorted her to the front desk, then returned to where Swan was making some notes in a file, exuding calm and satisfaction.

'You were surprised I agreed so readily?'

'Yes, sir, I suppose I was.'

'Why not? She's had some training, of a kind. There's no doubting her commitment to the cause. I suspect she's half-way to losing her mind, which could be a tremendous asset in some aspects of our work. Anyone prepared to throw their life away for an ideal – whether it's a country or a dead man she's still in love with – well, why not?'

'Are you thinking of the Salisbury business? You said you needed someone intelligent and unobtrusive.'

'Yes, and disposable. Could you organise her visas? And book her a ticket on tonight's BOAC flight to Montevideo.'

◊

Clemency had time to make one call before returning to Broadway. Even though it was almost six in Bern, Lucinda was still at her desk. Clemency reported on her meeting with Swan, and then there was silence.

'You know you can't trust him, don't you?' Lucinda said at last.

'Yes.'

'He's found this mission because he wants you out of the way. And he may not mind too much if that becomes permanent.'

'Yes.'

'Are you going to go?'

Clemency thought of Peter at the Czech border. He hadn't hesitated or doubted where his duty lay. He'd risked his life not only for his agent, but for her.

'I don't have a choice, do I?'

The End

Clemency White will return in
THE GIRL KNOWS NOTHING